Murder Under A Blue Moon

A Mona Moon Mystery
Book One

Abigail Keam

Worker Bee Press

The history is true as are the politicians, horsemen, and jockeys. The
1933 Kentucky Derby Race is one of the most famous horse races of
all time. The Moon family and Moon Manor are fabrications of my
imagination. So is Lord Farley—'tis a shame though.
Special thanks to Melanie Murphy.

ISBN 978 1 0946745 5 1
4 3 2019

Published in the USA

Worker Bee Press
P.O. Box 485
Nicholasville, KY 40340

1

Mona Moon picked up her dusty knapsack and battered valise, making her way down the ship's ramp where the New York City dock bristled with baggage porters, dock workers, cabbies, newspaper reporters, police, hustlers, and families welcoming loved-ones with flowers and kisses. There were no kisses and flowers for Mona. No loved-ones, tiptoeing and stretching their necks on the dock, searched for her. Mona was alone.

She hurried through customs, anxious to be off before all the cabs were snatched up. It was after midnight, and the last thing Mona wanted was to be stranded on a lonely pier.

Luckily, Mona was able to hail a taxi and give her address. "Chinatown," she muttered, sick with exhaustion. She had spent five months in Mesopotamia mapping the river systems emanating from the Zagros Mountains. Worn and thin from months of privation, Mona was ready for a hot bath, a clean bed, and a meal. Any kind of food would suffice. Then she wanted to hibernate in a deep sleep for several days.

It had been an arduous expedition fraught with danger. It was good that Mona always kept her pistol handy. It had saved her on many occasions—too many for her taste.

The cab screeched to a halt at Mona's address, and a sleepy driver let her out. He didn't bother to help her with the luggage as he disapproved of women wearing trousers instead of dresses.

Mona showed her disapproval of the cabby's disdain by withholding a tip. She briskly strode through the building's door and was out of earshot as the driver sneered, "This ain't no jitney, lady . . . oh, excuse me, you must be a sir, but who could tell?"

She climbed some rickety stairs leading to a little one-room apartment and unlocking the door, stumbled into her tiny efficiency, sighing with relief. Her room was as she left it with the exception of a stack of mail on a table, which acted as both desk and dining area, accompanied by one chair, one bookcase, and one single bed neatly made.

Mr. Zhang had come through for her, collecting her mail and dutifully saving it, even though she owed him back rent.

Mona set her luggage by the door and dove into the letters. She was expecting a letter and a fat check from the National Geographic Society, inviting her on their Amazon expedition.

She quickly perused the stack of letters, mostly bills, until she found one with the return address she was hoping for. Quickly tearing the envelope open, Mona read:

Dear Miss Moon,

Thank you for your application to join the Amazon expedition, which the National Geographic Society is funding some months from now. Even though your credentials and experience are quite impressive, we feel the Amazon expedition is not suitable for a woman, even for one as yourself with such superior attributes.

Please feel free to apply for another expedition where the day-to-day exertions would be less taxing for one of the fairer sex.

Best Regards,
Winston Banks

Mona let the letter fall to the floor. She was in deep trouble. Without the income from the upcoming Amazon expedition, Mona was in a financial crisis. She had three hundred dollars in her pocket out of which she had to pay back rent, buy food, and support herself until the next assignment materialized. Even though three hundred dollars was a princely sum during the Depression, it would not last long unless she could obtain another source of income between gigs in her field. Tomorrow, she would start looking in the paper for a job. Even a salesgirl's position sounded good at the moment. Times were hard, and one had to do what one had to do to survive.

A sharp knock on the door broke Mona's train of thought. Startled, she glanced at her wristwatch. It was close to two in the morning.

She grabbed the revolver from her purse. "Who is it?"

A man's voice filtered through the flimsy wooden door. "Am I speaking to Madeline Mona Moon?"

"Who wants to know?"

"My name is Dexter Deatherage. I'm a lawyer from Deatherage, Combs, and Sharp. I represent your Uncle Manfred Michael Moon's estate."

Throwing open the door, Mona pointed the revolver squarely at the man's forehead. "What do you want, Mr. Deatherage from Deatherage, Combs, and Sharp?"

Mr. Deatherage's eyes grew large as saucers, but he tried to quiet the quiver in his voice. He was a respectable man and was not used to having women point guns at him. "I have important business to discuss with you."

"At two in the morning?"

"I am sorry but I have waited a week. Your ship was late arriving, and I'm afraid time is of the essence. I was at the dock earlier and called out your name. Did you not hear?"

"Oh, was that you? I thought it might be a bill collector."

"Miss Moon, may I come in? I don't think we should be discussing our business in a public hallway."

"Drop the briefcase, turn around, and put your hands up against the wall."

Mr. Deatherage protested, "This is outrageous!"

Flicking the revolver at him, Mona ordered, "Do it, Bub, or else."

Seeing he had no choice, Mr. Deatherage put down his briefcase, turned, and put his hands high above his head against the wall.

Mona expertly patted down Mr. Deatherage's navy pinstriped double-breasted suit, paying special attention to any pockets and even ran her hand up the inseam of his trousers, eliciting a high-pitched whimper from the prim attorney. She took out his wallet and went through it, finding five hundred dollars in small bills, a driver's license, and a worn snapshot of a woman with two children, supposedly his family, plus New York restaurant receipts and a railroad ticket stub. Finding no weapons, she went through his leather case.

Mr. Deatherage started to turn, but Mona

barked, "Stay as you are." Seeing nothing suspicious, Mona put the gun in her pants pocket. "Okay, you can come in. I'm sorry, Mr. Deatherage, but a lady can't be too careful when a stranger knocks on her door in the middle of the night. Understand?"

The lawyer staggered inside and eased onto the apartment's one chair. "May I have a glass of water? I'm not used to this kind of treatment, especially when I bring glad tidings."

Curious, Mona was silent as she let the washbasin faucet run until the rusty-looking water turned clean before filling a chipped glass and handing it to Mr. Deatherage.

He looked askance at the glass before taking several sips. "That's better. Just give me a moment to compose myself." The lawyer took several deep breaths.

Mona sat quietly on her bed, watching Mr. Deatherage and wondering what his business had to do with her. He had stated he was bringing glad tidings. She could use some good news and patiently waited for him to speak.

Mr. Deatherage wiped his forehead with his linen monogrammed handkerchief before opening his briefcase and laying papers on the table. Clearing his throat, Mr. Deatherage straightened the knot in his tie and spoke in a loud firm voice, "Miss Moon, I'm here to inform you that your uncle, Manfred Michael Moon died two weeks ago. In accordance with his wishes and Last Will and Testament, Mr. Moon has bequeathed to you his property, all real and liquid assets, to be distributed immediately upon his death."

Looking up from his papers, Mr. Deatherage said, "Miss Moon, did you hear me? You are a very wealthy young lady. All you need to do is sign these papers and all will be yours. There are only a few stipulations. One is you must take up residence at Moon Manor, the family residence in Lexington, Kentucky, and use it as your permanent domicile. All property, real and liquid, must stay within the bloodline of the Moon family upon the event of your demise, which excludes any husband you might acquire along the way, and any offspring of yours must maintain the Moon moniker as their surname."

Mr. Deatherage peered over his papers. "You don't have any husbands tucked away, do you?"

"I've never married."

"Betrothed?"

"Been too busy making a living to have time for romance."

"Any entanglements I should know about?"

"Look around. I don't even have a plant."

The lawyer seemed relieved. "At least, we don't have any inconvenient domestic details to muddy the waters."

"You say I'm wealthy. How much money are we talking about?"

"I don't have the exact figures with me, but you will never have to work another day in your life, and your inheritance comes to you debt free. Mr. Moon was very frugal, but scrupulous about paying his bills. I wish all my clients were like him. Mr. Moon left his affairs as tidy as one could hope for in a patron."

Mona was taken back by this information. "Why would my uncle leave me the Moon fortune when my father was disowned by the family because of his marriage to my mother?"

Mr. Deatherage winced. "I was hoping that unhappy bit of history would not raise its ugly head."

"How could it not?"

"You're quite right. There are some bequests for his sister, your Aunt Melanie and her children, but the rest is yours. All you need to do is sign these papers." He retrieved a Parker Duofold fountain pen from his coat pocket and held it out to her.

Skeptical, Mona said, "I'm not sure."

"Miss Moon, I don't understand your reluctance. I assure you this inheritance is aboveboard. Don't you want to be wealthy, and get out of this rabbit warren of an apartment building?" Mr. Deatherage looked about the shabby room.

"I can't forget how my father lost his inheritance, and the curt brush-off my mother got from the Moon family when Father died."

"That is not entirely correct, Miss Moon. I know for a fact your uncle underwrote your education."

"My father's annuity from his maternal grandmother paid for my education."

"No, Miss Moon. Your uncle paid for your college education. I would know because I wrote the checks myself."

"How could my mother not have told me?"

"She was sworn to secrecy by your uncle. He wanted to undo the enmity between your father and the Moon family, but had to wait until Moon senior had died to make amends. Unfortunately by that time, your father had passed on as well."

"Yet my uncle was content to have my mother live a life of toil when he could have easily summoned us both back to Moon Manor."

"That would not have been possible, Miss Moon. Even you can see that. It would have put the Moon family in a very awkward situation socially. Of course, society is not as strict now as it was thirty years ago."

"It isn't?"

"All the principal characters involved in your parents' scandal are now deceased, except for your aunt. Being a mid-life child, she was very young at the time of your parents' marriage, and not really connected to your father since he was so much older."

"Why didn't Uncle Michael leave her the Moon fortune?"

"I'd rather not say."

"Ah, come on, Mr. Deatherage. You're among friends."

Forgetting discretion, Mr. Deatherage leaned forward and whispered, "He couldn't stand her—his own sister. Very bad business there."

"But why me? It doesn't make sense."

"Mr. Moon kept watch over you through the years. He was pleased that you graduated from college with honors and of your exploits as a cartographer and explorer. He was proud, Miss Moon. Very proud. I think he wanted to right all the wrongs done to you and your mother."

"I don't know. The whole thing sounds fishy."

"Miss Moon, I'm very tired. I will leave the papers with you to peruse. If you sign, you will become one of the richest women in the country. Think of what you could do. You could under-write your own expeditions. And there is a loophole. If for some reason you wish to relinquish your position as head of the Moon fortune after presiding over Moon Manor, you may turn over the responsibility to your aunt and live on a stipend provided in the will."

"I see."

"Please sign, Miss Moon. I wish to go to my hotel and sleep. It is way past my usual bedtime, and I'm exhausted as you must be as well, but if you insist, I will call tomorrow expecting your answer." Mr. Deatherage rose, gathering his briefcase.

Mona glanced around the pathetic efficiency. She had worked her fingers to the bone since graduating college, gaining respect and accolades for her work, but this was as far as she had gotten in life—a run-down apartment, scraping for every dime, and now no immediate employment due to some outdated prejudice of a Winston Banks because of her gender. The idea she might have money to finance her own expeditions was intriguing, and there was that clause to release her from any obligation if Moon Manor turned out to be a bust. "Just a minute, Mr. Deatherage. You're right. I have nothing to lose, but everything to gain. May I borrow your pen?"

"Assuredly, Miss Moon," Mr. Deatherage answered, handing over the fountain pen. "You won't regret this."

"I'd better not, or you'll be the first person on my list."

"List?"

"I think you know what I mean."

13

Mr. Deatherage did indeed. After all, he was from Kentucky where folks still settled grievances with a gun. He had been hoping Miss Moon was of a different temperament, but apparently the apple hadn't fallen far from the tree, so to speak.

Mona Moon's little revolver had proven that.

2

Mona and Mr. Deatherage had traveled for several days when they descended from a train onto a platform on the newly opened Union Terminal in Cincinnati. Mona was astounded at the size of its rotunda and the gleaming mosaics adorning the walls.

"This was built during the Depression?" she gasped.

"Amazing, isn't it? The dome of the rotunda is 106 feet high. The murals are made of glass tiles. The two main murals represent the history of the United States and of Cincinnati. The others represent industry in Cincinnati."

"The murals are unbelievable. They even compare to the great works of art I saw in Mesopotamia. The ancient peoples there liked to work with glazed bricks—reminds me very much of these mosaics."

"The entire station can accommodate seventeen thousand people and over two hundred trains a day."

They stood back-to-back admiring the larger than life glass murals on the walls while throngs of passengers and porters either disappeared down the sprawling concourse or hurried outside to catch a cab.

"If you appreciate this, wait until you see the hotel I've booked us into—the Netherland. It's decorated in Art Deco and is stunning," Mr. Deatherage stated, trying to ignore the curious stares of people who gaped at Mona's attire. She was wearing tight ankle-length black pants with a white shirt accompanied by a short black and red jacket and black ballet slippers. A beret adorned her head. She looked like a confused French matador.

Mr. Deatherage had struggled with Mona's choice of attire on the trip, especially once they got out of New York. The other women on the train were dressed to the nines, but Mona's eccentric clothes were far too attention getting. In fact, a little boy on the train asked Mona if she was from the circus. The exasperated attorney gently suggested selecting outfits a little more conservative from her wardrobe, but Mona paid him no heed.

Cincinnati was the last train stop before Lexington, and Mr. Deatherage wanted to give Mona a chance to get her bearings and fix herself up before arriving in the Bluegrass, but Mona ignored his suggestions. However, his opening came when the manager of the Netherland Hotel insisted Mona wear an evening gown when dining at the fashionable Palm Court.

Mr. Deatherage threw down the gauntlet. Either Mona purchase women's clothing and have her hair coiffed, or he was leaving her to the devices of the Moon family by herself. He was tired of being embarrassed by Mona's unconventional appearance, and worried she would be a laughing stock among her peers in Lexington. The matador pants had to go!

Mona's clothes consisted of thrift shop finds or cheap native clothing purchased on her adventures. In other words, she had to make do with what she had. Besides, her work called for sturdy functional clothing and work boots. Fancy threads were just a waste of money, but that didn't mean Mona didn't appreciate beautiful apparel.

Realizing she could finally purchase quality clothing, Mona feigned offense and pouted until she was out of Mr. Deatherage's view, not wanting to give him the satisfaction of seeing her drool at the thought of shopping. She bounded to the lobby and asked the clerk at the front desk where the *swells* shopped.

"Well, young lady, the women in society shop at an establishment called Gidding-Jenny. If you go out this hallway to the street, make two rights. You will see a sign for the dress shop. Can't miss it."

Mona thanked him and dashed out of the hotel. Before she knew it, Mona was lounging on a plush settee, sipping hot tea as models paraded the latest fashions for her approval.

Still not able to throw off her conservative spending habits, she settled on simple day frocks, blouses, sweaters, jackets, evening gowns, gloves, stockings, shoes, slips, dressing gowns, purses, and unmentionables of the finest quality, but only two of each. Even then, Mona thought she was being extravagant but relished the colors and textures of silk, satin, tulle, velvet, lace, and taffeta.

Triumphant, Mona returned to the hotel, trailed by a small caravan of stock boys loaned out by Gidding-Jenny, carrying the boon of parcels and boxes. Marching to her suite, she happened to glance in a hallway mirror and froze at the state of her hair. It was a blousy halo surrounding a red face peeling from a sunburn acquired in the Mesopotamian sun. She couldn't help but frown at the condition of her calloused hands, highlighted by nails, rough-looking and chipped. Mona gave a little groan. Her hands certainly gave away the fact she made her living by manual labor, not that she was ashamed by any means, but her appearance betrayed she had been down on her luck. Mona certainly didn't want to give her relatives this first impression.

Luckily, the hotel had a beauty parlor where Mona had her platinum hair permed and styled, nails painted, and enjoyed a soothing facial, which calmed the redness of the sunburn. And for the pièce de résistance, Mona had her face professionally made-up. Mona especially liked her lipstick choice, which matched the color of her nails—Jungle Red.

That evening she entered the two-storied Palm Court of the Netherland Hotel wearing a slinky, champagne-colored, backless, slipper satin gown, which outlined her curves leaving almost nothing to the imagination, causing men's heads to swivel.

Even Mr. Deatherage did a double take before standing and welcoming Mona to his table. "My goodness," was all the gentleman could utter, after clearing his throat. "My goodness."

"Settle down, frat boy," said a middle-aged woman wearing a black sequined hat placed jauntily on her head. The woman stuck out her hand. "Hello. My name is Wilhelmina Deatherage, but everyone calls me Willie. I'm Dexter's wife."

Mona shook hands with Willie while Mr. Deatherage scooted in Mona's chair. Though she was surprised to see Mrs. Deatherage, she didn't show it. "Very nice to meet you."

"Likewise. Dexter telegraphed me saying you might need help in the dolling-up department, making me think you were a Bug-eyed Betty, but from all the men staring, I think you've done okay on your own. You got some chassis—a regular Sheba. Not many women could wear a dress like that."

"Thank you. I've known how to dress myself for a long time now." Mona raised an eyebrow at Willie's chatter.

"And your hair. You have the Moon hair. Platinum—just like Jean Harlow."

"Who?" Mona asked.

"Jean Harlow. The famous movie actress. Her hair is like yours—that strange white. A curious color. Neither blonde nor gray and not really white. Platinum."

Mona gave a confused look.

"Oh, I'm sorry, my dear. You've been gone from the States a long time."

"Yes, I have, but then I rarely go to the movies. I'm usually working."

"Well, Jean Harlow is all the rage these days, and you are the spitting image of her."

Mona smiled. "I must check Miss Harlow out and see one of her movies."

"And your eyes. I see you have the Moon

amber eyes. Dexter, why didn't you tell me Miss Moon was so hotsy-totsy?"

Being used to strangers making comments about her hair and fair skin, Mona said, "Yes, I know the Moon family has a history of albinism. I certainly exhibit traits of it."

"Must be," Willie noted, staring at Mona's hair "You have the *it* look. Simply the cat's meow."

Even in the restaurant's dim light, Mona could see Mr. Deatherage was blushing. "Ignore my wife's patter. She's addicted to mystery novels, especially American hardboilers, and likes to talk like Sam Spade, or in off days, Peter Wimsey."

"Peter Wimsey is a lord and British. Not American at all," Willie said. She drew a mono-grammed sterling silver cigarette case from her beaded purse, offering Mona a cigarette.

Mona politely refused.

Willie withdrew a cigarette, and by the time she held it to her lips, Mr. Deatherage had produced a gold plated lighter. "Did you finish your shopping, dear?"

"I bought a few things. That reminds me. Since I didn't have any money, I had the store add the clothing bill to the hotel. I hope it's all right. I wasn't sure how much to spend, so I hope I didn't go over my budget."

Willie chuckled. "Honey, you can buy anything your little heart desires and more."

"Now dear, let's be more cautious saying such things to Miss Moon. I've seen plenty of heirs who squandered their wealth only to end up penniless and out on the street."

"Oh, tosh. Miss Moon doesn't look like a foolish young woman. Arc you, honey?"

"I don't think I'm a foolish person, although getting comfortable with spending money freely will take some getting use to—happily I might add."

Willie inhaled deeply and exhaled a plume of smoke, which engulfed the entire table. Dexter Deatherage coughed and waved the smoke away from his face. His wife appeared not to notice. "I was very glad to have Dexter wire me to join the two of you. I missed him terribly while he was in New York, waiting for your ship to arrive, and I was curious to meet you. I've never met a woman cartographer before."

"Well, you've seen me. What's your take?"

"I was worried that you were a flash in the

pan, one of those mawkish waifs always with their heads in books whom my poor Dexter was going to have to save every time he turned around."

"But you don't now?"

Willie stubbed out her cigarette and appraised Mona. "I think you will be able to hold your own with the Moon family."

"Are they so vicious?"

"Your father was your grandfather's favorite son, yet he was spurned when he married your mother without so much a second thought from your grandfather. How do I put this? Your aunt favors your grandfather."

"I see."

Dexter nervously tugged at his starched collar and quickly intervened to reassure Mona. "Now, Willie dear, you mustn't utter such things. Miss Moon will think badly of her family before she even meets them."

"Bully for her."

"Please, Mr. Deatherage. Is there something I need to know? I would rather not walk into Moon Manor without having been briefed on every aspect of my inheritance."

Willie leaned forward. "Your Aunt Melanie is contesting the will."

"Does Aunt Melanie have a case?"

"Not really as long as you don't give her any cause."

"Meaning?"

"No gambling. No men. No scandalous behavior. There's a morals clause in the will."

"I wish you had told me earlier. I wouldn't have bought such a bold dress," Mona said, glimpsing down at her plunging neckline.

Willie teased, "Ignore Dexter on moral turpitude. Dexter is such a bluenose, he thinks spitting on the sidewalk is a crime."

"It is," Dexter complained, signaling to a waiter. "It spreads TB."

Willie nudged her husband with her elbow. "See what I mean, Mona, but I love him, God help the poor sod."

He smiled and blew a kiss to his wife before ordering appetizers. "I wish we could order a cocktail."

Willie clutched Dexter's hand reassuringly. "I think President Roosevelt intends to rid us of Prohibition."

"Not if the Southern Baptists have anything to say about it," Mr. Deatherage mumbled.

"You do know the new president is Franklin D. Roosevelt?" Willie asked.

"I may not know who Jean Harlow is, but I did keep up with national news. Even in Mesopotamia, there were radios," Mona said.

"I guess you could drink your fill in Mesopotamia?" Willie said, taking a little silver flask out of her purse.

"Mesopotamians are Muslims. They don't drink hard spirits," replied Mona, refusing the flask.

"Pity," Willie reflected while pouring hooch in her tea. She looked up at Mona's confused expression. "A little giggle juice of my own. It's good old Kentucky bourbon. Bootlegged, of course."

"Ah," was all Mona said.

Mr. Deatherage jumped in the conversation. "Liquor is one thing you don't have to worry about. Moon Manor has a full compliment of wine and spirits. When your Uncle Manfred saw Prohibition was going to become law in 1920, he bought out entire liquor stores and went to local distilleries to purchase Kentucky bourbon. You know Kentucky used to be the country's leading wine maker besides making the finest bourbon."

"I did not," Mona replied, unfolding her napkin. "Shall we order now?"

Willie held up her teacup. "First, let's have a toast. Here's to Madeline Mona Moon. May she overcome the prejudice, hatred, and backbiting, which are the traits of the Moon family and bring some fresh air into that stuffy old dynasty. Here's to your success, honey."

Dexter reluctantly clicked his water glass against the teacup and looked expectantly at Mona.

Mona smiled and held up her glass. "I'll drink to that," she said cheerfully, oh so happy her revolver was close at hand in her clutch purse.

If Willie Deatherage was correct in her assessment of the Moon family, her revolver might come in handy for the future.

Oh dear! What was she walking into?

3

Mona Moon stepped off the train at the Lexington Depot, while Dexter Deatherage beckoned a cab.

Willie Deatherage grabbed Mona's hand. "Honey, Dexter is sending me home, so you have only my capable husband to help you fend off the maniacal clutches of your family who await you at Moon Manor. Don't show fear and you'll do fine." She kissed Mona on the cheek before climbing into the cab. "See you at home soon, Dexter."

"As quickly as I can, Sweet Willie, but it may be awhile."

Willie blew her husband a kiss before telling the cab driver to take her home.

Dexter watched the cab until it turned onto

Broadway, and then motioned to a gleaming red and black Daimler, pulling up alongside Mona. A black man in a maroon uniform with brass buttons jumped out and opened the door for Mona after tipping the bill of his hat.

"This is Jamison," Mr. Deatherage said. "He's your chauffeur."

"Yes, Miss, I'll take you anywhere you want to go. I used to drive carriages for Mr. Moon senior. That was a long way back, but I can drive anything—tractor, mule plows, horses, cars, pony carts. You tie a pig to a wagon, and I can drive it. Something wrong, Miss? You look a *mite* peaked."

"No, it's just I wasn't expecting a chauffeur. I thought I would take a cab."

"That wouldn't be fittin', and make me look bad, Miss."

"I see."

"I'll help Miss Moon into the car, Jamison. You see to her trunks."

"Yes, sir."

Mr. Deatherage helped Mona into the Daimler and climbed in, shutting the car door.

"Jamison is a good employee. He's sharp as a tack and is aware of everything going on in the

Moon household. You would be wise to use him. My advice is to take it slow with the staff. They are used to doing things a certain way, and it would cause them great anxiety to have someone new challenge their ways."

"Don't upset the apple cart in other words."

Mr. Deatherage grinned. "At least, not in the first week. Let everyone get to know you."

"So they have faith in me?"

"In a way. They will want to know there is a steady hand at the helm."

"I understand, Mr. Deatherage. You forget that I have worked with many peoples of different faiths and cultures. I know how to get along."

"That's a great asset, but you must remember Kentucky may have stayed in the Union during the Civil War but Lexington is a Southern town. The Bluegrass aristocracy believe the South won the war. Everyone has his place, and woe to anyone who tries to change things. After all, you are from New York. You're a big city Yankee."

Mona sighed. She understood how the world worked, but that didn't mean she liked it. "I grasp your meaning, Mr. Deatherage."

Jamison jumped into the front seat, and Mr.

Deatherage tapped on the partition with his cane. Jamison drove through Lexington as Mona looked out the window at what seemed a prosperous small town with stylish stores, graceful brick homes, movie palaces, and institutions of higher learning such as Transylvania University and the University of Kentucky. Educated, intelligent people lived here, or so Mona hoped.

He proudly drove down grand boulevards lined with giant pin oak trees until he pulled onto a country lane where Thoroughbred, Saddlebred, and Standardbred farms straddled the road.

"Looks a lot like Ireland," Mona commented, rolling down her window to get a better view. "And smells divine."

Mr. Deatherage said, "Everyone says that. I guess that's why so many Irish were drawn here."

"Who built these rock walls?"

"The Irish at first. They taught the slaves who built them later. That's why we call them slave walls. All dry stacked limestone without mortar. We're trying to convince landowners to save them. Many are tearing them down and using the rocks for other purposes."

"They're so beautiful. Does Mooncrest Farm

have slave walls?"

"Miles and miles of them."

"Wonderful. Are we near?"

"We've been passing Mooncrest Farm for several minutes now."

"Really? Which side?"

"Both sides."

Mona blinked. "How many acres do I own?"

"A little over four thousand."

Astounded, Mona sat back in her seat. "What is the average size of a horse farm here?"

"Four or five hundred acres. That was too small for your grandfather, so he purchased the surrounding farms."

"How many employees are there?"

"About one hundred, not including the house staff."

"How many horses do I own?"

"Don't know how many you own personally. You have to ask your farm manager, Hugh Beaumont, for that information, but I do know over twelve hundred horses board on Mooncrest Farm."

"That's a lot of manure," Mona said, laughing.

"You will find Mooncrest Farm one of the

most beautiful horse farms in the world, and you are its mistress."

"I'm impressed. The upkeep of a farm like this costs a great deal of money. I know the Moon family dabbles in mining."

"It comes from copper, my dear. I thought you knew."

"My parents never discussed the Moon finances, but Mother regaled me with stories of the farm and the gardens her father planted. Father never talked much about his family. Copper from where?"

"Utah. New Mexico. Even Chile. Your great, great grandfather was a gold prospector and gave his son the deed to a worthless mine, or so he thought. Copper was discovered and in great industrial demand. Still is. Your great grandfather built the empire, and your grandfather expanded it during the Great War."

Mona understood. "You mean my grandfather was a war profiteer. Made money from the suffering of others," she commented bitterly.

Mr. Deatherage didn't respond at first, thinking of how to reply. Who was he to judge when his retainer came from the Moon fortune made by war investments? "Perhaps you may do better with the family's wealth, Miss Moon."

Mona admired the horses grazing in beautiful green fields guarded by gleaming white fences. "I intend to," she murmured. "I certainly intend to."

4

The Daimler turned left and stopped before a twelve-foot-high wrought iron gate. Two huge stone columns supported statues of lions attacking frightened gazelles.

"Not very welcoming are they?" Mona commented on the statues.

"I don't think they're meant to be," Mr. Deatherage replied.

"Family mascots, huh?"

Mr. Deatherage chuckled. "The Moon family is never subtle with its imagery. You know up front you're dealing with predators. Oh, maybe I shouldn't have said that."

"Like Daniel to the lion's den, I see."

"Everyone from the older generation is dead, and Miss Melanie, well, she's more flighty than mean. I'm sure we can settle this lawsuit matter as soon as she is reassured you won't be wrenching her annual stipend and privileges away from her. She's reacting out of fear. It was a shock when Melanie discovered she wasn't the main heir. We all thought Miles, her son, would eventually be master of Mooncrest Farm. The lawsuit is just a knee jerk reaction."

"I hope you're right."

Jamison honked the horn and a man ran out from a stone guardhouse and opened the gate. As the car passed, the man tipped his hat.

Mona turned around in her seat and watched him close the heavy gates.

"That's Burl," Mr. Deatherage said. "His grandfather was born a slave on this estate."

Mona said, "The roots of the employees go back deep."

"Very. Some are descendants of slaves who came with the original white pioneers. They take their duties seriously and can be trusted, even though they consider the Moons to be mere interlopers. Owners of the estate come and go, but these people stay. They are deeply invested in the land."

Mona squared back her shoulders, glancing at Mr. Deatherage. As her employee, could he be trusted? Mona would find out soon enough, and if her extended family had any delusions she was a namby-pamby, they would soon find out differently as well. She had worked in some of the most inhospitable places in the world and had emerged unscathed with both her virtue and pay intact, but she would need someone who had her back in this instance. Was that someone Mr. Deatherage?

She pushed those thoughts from her mind as the car continued up a tree-lined drive and finally rounded a curve, where a large lake shimmered in the midday sun. A cheerful geyser sprouted happily into the air before a stone mansion.

Mona couldn't help but gasp.

Her mother had shown her pictures of Moon Manor, but the photographs did not do justice to the mansion. It could be compared to English manors such as Benham Park or Eaton Hall, at both of which Mona had been a weekend guest.

Moon Manor was a square mansion built in the Georgian style. It was three stories high with a stone balustrade, traversing the roofline. Four broad marble steps led up to a covered portico supported by four stone Corinthian columns. Another pair of imposing marble lions guarded the front door.

"Impressive isn't it," Mr. Deatherage said.

"I own this?"

"Lock, stock, and barrel. The deed of the house and the land has already been recorded in your name. It's yours."

Jamison followed the drive to the front portico and eased to a stop in front of a line of people in uniforms waiting. He slid open the partition, saying, "Miss Moon, you're home."

"Thank you, Jamison."

"Anytime you need me, just call the kitchen. That's where I'll be if not in the garage. I'll be happy to take you anywhere. I can drive anything. You just pick the car, and I'll drive it for you."

"We have more than one car?"

"Yes'am. Lots of them."

Mona took a deep breath. This new life was going to take some getting used to, but she mustn't show she was nervous.

Jamison jumped out and opened her door.

Mona stepped out and was greeted by a woman wearing a heavily starched, blue striped dress and a pince-nez. A fob watch was pinned to her dress and her belt sagged under the weight of a brass key ring, which held over a dozen keys of various sizes. The woman's graying auburn hair was pulled so tightly into a bun the skin on her face seemed stretched. Mona took her to be the housekeeper and took an instant dislike to the woman's severe appearance.

She reminded Mona of a riverboat captain who had once guided her down the Mississippi, while spewing talk about his piety during dinner, and then tried to accost her after dessert. She was glad there had been a doctor onboard. The captain needed one after she finished with him. This woman had the same pinched look as the captain. It turned Mona's stomach.

Mr. Deatherage came around behind Mona and warned, "Mrs. Haggin is the housekeeper. She's your Aunt Melanie's creature."

"Welcome to Moon Manor, Miss Moon," Mrs. Haggin said in a voice as heavily starched as her uniform.

"Thank you."

"May I introduce the staff?"

"By all means."

"This is Thomas, the butler, and his staff Samuel and Isaac."

Thomas stepped forward and said, "We hope to make your stay with us comfortable."

Your stay with us? Mona thought. "I'm sure you and your staff will exceed my expectation."

If Thomas noticed the bite in Mona's remark, he didn't show it. He stepped back into line.

"This is Monsieur Bisaillon. He is the cook."

Monsieur Bisaillon crisply bowed his head. "Enchanté, Mademoiselle. You must tell me if you have any special requests concerning the menus."

"I look forward to your expert guidance in such matters, Monsieur Bisaillon. I'm entirely in your capable hands."

The cook bowed again, feeling relieved that his position as head chef was secure. "May I introduce you to Obadiah and Jedediah, my assistants."

"Nice to meet you both. Are you two brothers?"

Obadiah spoke, "Yes, Miss Moon. Twins."

"Your parents must have loved the Bible.

Obadiah is the shortest book in the Bible, is it not? Refers to a prophet during the Assyrian Period."

"Yes, Miss," Obadiah answered.

"If I remember my Biblical Hebrew, it means 'one who serves God.'"

"It surely does."

"And Jedediah. That was the second blessing name given to Solomon by the prophet Nathan. Your name means 'friend of God.'"

Jedediah asked, "You a Bible reader, Miss Moon?"

"I keep my hand in."

Obadiah said, "No need to be formal with us, Miss. Folks call us Obbie and Jed."

"I'll try to remember."

Mrs. Haggin continued down the line. "This is Violet, your personal maid."

Mona was startled learning she was to have her own maid, but said nothing and maintained her poker face.

Violet curtsied and spoke, "Nice to meet you, Miss. I hope I will be able to meet your standards."

"I'm sure you will, Violet."

"This is Dora, the downstairs senior maid."

Dora nodded her head. "Miss."

"Dora, nice to meet you."

"This is Mabelle, the upstairs maid."

"Mabelle. A good hello."

"Miss." Mabelle gave a quick curtsy.

"This is Mr. Gallo, our gardener."

Mr. Gallo doffed his hat and spoke with a strong Italian accent. "I knew your grandpapa, Miss." Seeing the strong disapproving look on Mrs. Haggin's face, he looked away.

"I was hoping to meet someone who knew my mother's father. You must show me the gardens. My mother told me the original design of the garden was his," Mona said, referring to her maternal grandfather.

Mr. Gallo smiled brightly. "I helped plant many trees here including the great black oak trees. They are native to Kentucky."

"They line the driveway, do they not? I noticed the reddish leaves."

Mr. Gallo's face beamed as he spoke. "Your grandpapa and I placed those beauties in the ground some forty years ago."

"I look forward to taking a tour of the farm

with you, Mr. Gallo."

"Yes, Miss Moon. Anytime. Anytime."

Moving down the line, Mrs. Haggin continued the introductions. "This is Archer. He was your uncle's valet."

"What is your position now, Mr. Archer?"

"It's simply Archer when the Moon family addresses me, Miss," the valet said, correcting Mona. "I now tend to young Miles."

Mona did not like Archer correcting her in front of the staff, but said nothing, turning to Mr. Deatherage.

"So you'll be leaving Moon Manor then, Archer?" Mr. Deatherage asked.

"No, sir, not since Mr. Miles has taken up residence in Moon Manor."

Shock must have shown on Mr. Deatherage's face, as the rest of the staff looked down at their feet. Only Archer and Mrs. Haggin showed no sign of shame or embarrassment.

"Steady on, man," Mona murmured to Mr. Deatherage. She casually asked, "Has anyone else taken up residence in Moon Manor, Mrs. Haggin?"

"Your Aunt Melanie and your cousins, young

Miles and Miss Meredith," she replied coldly.

Mona's eyebrows rose a bit. "Please introduce me to the rest of the staff." Mona numbly followed Mrs. Haggin, barely listening to her prattle as Mona considered the implications of her relatives taking advantage of her uncle's demise to move into Moon Manor. As Mona understood it, her aunt had a large house of her own on the estate.

The first volley of resistance had been fired. Her aunt and cousins obviously assumed Mona was a pushover and would take flight at the first sign of aggression. They had seriously erred if they thought they could chase Mona away. They weren't dealing with a lamb, but with a lioness.

It was time for Mona to teach them that she could kill gazelles as well.

5

Mona climbed past the imposing lion statues guarding the broad marble steps of the portico.

Mr. Deatherage said, "Allow me, Miss Moon," as he opened the massive front door. "Welcome to Moon Manor. May your new home bring joy."

The mistress of Moon Manor swept around him into a mahogany paneled foyer with a grand staircase on the right leading to the second floor balcony. Mona stopped and took in her surroundings, taking an immediate dislike to the room. *I hope the rest of the house isn't such a gloomy gus*, she thought.

Mrs. Haggin followed Mr. Deatherage into the foyer. "The family is waiting for you in the drawing room, Miss."

"Whom would that be, Mrs. Haggin?" Mona

asked, shedding her new driving gloves.

"Your Aunt Melanie and your cousins."

"Please convey my apologies to them. The journey here has been very taxing. I am tired and wish to retire. We can meet at dinner tonight. Would you escort me to my room please?"

Mrs. Haggin looked quite vexed. "But Miss Moon!"

"I wish to be escorted to my room please. NOW!"

"Very well, then. I'll have one of the boys bring in your trunks."

Mona turned to Mr. Deatherage so Mrs. Haggin couldn't see her face. "Shall I be expecting you and Willie at dinner tonight?" She mouthed, *please come*.

"We would be delighted," Mr. Deatherage answered, secretly miffed he wouldn't be spending his first evening at home, but Mona Moon was his most important client.

When Mrs. Haggin started up the staircase, Mr. Deatherage sidled up to Mona and whispered, "Well played, Miss Moon. Make them dance to your tune." He was out the door in a flash, jauntily donning his gray Homburg and whistling a tune down the portico steps.

Jamison waited for him beside the Daimler.

"Home, Jamison," Mr. Deatherage said. Saluting Moon Manor, Mr. Deatherage mumbled, "A lioness has returned home."

"What's that, sir?"

"The lion of Moon Manor has returned home, Jamison. Miss Moon has inherited her father's disposition."

Jamison murmured, "She's gonna need it. With that bunch, Miss Moon's sure gonna need it."

"Amen to that, Jamison. Amen to that."

6

The housekeeper showed Mona to a bedroom down the end of a dark hallway.

Mona strode in and stood quietly. It had been recently cleaned, and the scent of freshly washed linens wafted about the room, but it still looked dingy. There were no vases filled with flowers or even a fruit basket welcoming her. The wallpaper looked like it hadn't been changed since the turn of the century.

Mrs. Haggin opened a door. "This room is en suite. You have both shower and tub. No closet but the room does have an ample wardrobe."

Mona looked out the small window. The view was of several buildings in need of repair and paint. "Surely, this is not the master suite."

Mrs. Haggin looked surprised. "Well, no Miss.

Your aunt has moved into the master suite. She thought this room would be suitable for you. It's quite cozy, and is one of the quietest rooms in the manor."

Mona's eyes flashed as she swirled around to confront Mrs. Haggin. Her face must have been fierce, as Mrs. Haggin seemed startled.

"Be advised, Mrs. Haggin. I don't do cozy. Show me the master suite, please."

"Shall I send for your Aunt Melanie?"

"That won't be necessary."

"I must notify her, Miss. We can't intrude. It would be an invasion of Miss Melanie's privacy."

"Show me the master bedroom immediately, or you'll find yourself in search of employment elsewhere without references."

The housekeeper jerked her hand up over her heart. "Goodness. It's not my place to correct."

Mona cut in. "Then don't."

"Very well, but I must protest."

"Noted. After you."

Mona was led down the hall to the west wing of the house. They passed the wide staircase and a small closet, which housed an elevator. The housekeeper opened the first door on the right and held it open for Mona.

Mona was staggered by what she saw. The room was bright and airy with fresh flower arrangements adorning newly waxed mahogany tables with marble tops. A French Deco mirror, reaching to the ceiling, accented a marble fireplace ablaze with an inviting, crackling fire.

On the outside wall were massive windows and glass French doors, which led to a balcony spanning the length of the master bedroom allowing a great deal of light. Mona peered down into the gardens and observed Mr. Gallo with several helpers pruning topiary of horses, dogs, rabbits, and odd geometrical shapes. Beyond the garden were pastures with horses gamboling on the lush carpet of the Bluegrass, and in the distance were shiny rooftops of the barns and stables.

A door was slightly open. Mona pulled on the door handle only to discover the master bath. She stepped inside the spacious room whose walls and floor were made from green and white marble. The toilet seat was carved from a dark green marble, as was the bathtub. All fixtures were shiny with light reflecting the color of gold.

"Are these fixtures solid gold?"

"No, Miss. They are brass plated in gold. The architect didn't feel solid gold would hold up."

Mona nodded and continued exploring. The shower was encased in glass. Beside the toilet was a bidet. "Very European," Mona murmured, opening another door in the bathroom leading to a dressing room with mirrored closets lining two walls.

Following another door, Mona stepped into a small bedroom with a door leading to the main hallway. *Must be the maid's room,* she thought.

Coming back through the rooms, she paused when she saw Mrs. Haggin hugging the doorway. "The bath is larger than the room you showed me, Mrs. Haggin."

"I'm sorry the choice of your bedroom displeases you, Miss Moon."

"It does, indeed, which is why you are going to have Aunt Melanie's things packed up immediately and have my trunks brought up here."

"That seems an unreasonable request."

"I want my trunks carefully unpacked, and Aunt Melanie's possessions out of here within one half hour. Tell Violet to come up here immediately, and after you see to this, tell the family I will receive them at cocktails. What time is dinner?"

Pursing her lips, Mrs. Haggin replied, "Eight, Miss."

"Very well. I will meet them at seven thirty."

"Where shall I put Miss Melanie's things, Miss?"

"Doesn't she have her own house on the estate?"

"Yes."

"Tell Jamison to take her things back to her house," Mona said, giving Mrs. Haggin a severe look. "That goes for my cousins as well."

"Very well, Miss."

"Oh, one more thing, Mrs. Haggin. How many keys for this room?"

"Two Miss. I have one, and Miss Melanie has the other."

Mona held out her hand. "May I have the key please?"

"What? I need the key for the staff."

"Please give me your key and get the other key from my aunt. Give it to Violet. She's to have it when she comes up. After my trunks arrive, the only person allowed in this room is Violet. Understand?"

"Yes."

"You have your instructions, Mrs. Haggin."

"Yes, Miss."

Mona saw a glint of revulsion in Mrs. Haggin's eyes. Perhaps she was making a mistake. Didn't Mr. Deatherage warn her to make changes slowly? However, she knew enough of the world to know when a battle was ensuing.

Aunt Melanie's appropriation of the master suite was the first volley in what promised to be an all out war. If Mona didn't dig in now, she would be bullied by her relatives. She had to demonstrate that she was the head of the family now, and they had to yield to her dictates—not the other way around.

Power wasn't given. It was taken—by force if necessary.

Mona had learned that a long time ago.

7

"You asked for me, Miss Moon?" Violet said, standing in the doorway.

Angry shouting could be heard floating up the staircase.

"Yes, please shut the door."

Before Violet could close the door, a standard white poodle pushed past Violet and sat before Mona whimpering.

"Who is this?" Mona asked, scratching the dog behind the ears.

"Moon Manor has lots of dogs, but she was Mr. Manfred's favorite. She's been awfully blue since your uncle's death."

"What's her name?"

"Chloe."

"Has anyone in the family claimed her?"

"She was supposed to be put in the kennel before your arrival. I'll put her out."

"No, leave her. I like dogs. She'll be fine."

"If you say so, Miss."

"Do you have the key?"

"Yes, Miss."

"Are there only two keys to this room?"

"I think so, Miss."

"I want you to keep one key on you at all times. You are to guard it closely. Give it to no one, and keep it in a safe place on your person."

Violet looked puzzled but nodded.

"I will keep the other key with me as well. This room and the adjoining maid's room will be locked at all times. Do you understand?"

"Yes, Miss, but how will Mabelle clean?"

"She won't. You will."

"Oh," Violet sighed unhappily, as a lady's maid didn't usually clean.

"Your duties are going to change. No one is allowed into this suite except you and me. You are to take care of my rooms and my clothes. Does this key fit all the locks for this bedroom and the maid's room?"

"Yes, Miss Moon."

"Does this key fit other locks in the house?"

"Not to my knowledge, Miss. Each bedroom has its own key."

"Very well. Each time you go out of my rooms, you will lock the door. Each time you enter these rooms to work, you will lock the door behind you. Understood?"

"Yes, Miss." Violet jumped when a knock sounded at the door. "That must be Samuel and Isaac with your trunks."

"Let them in. Then lock the door. Show them to the bathroom and dressing room. Get my aunt's things out of here."

Violet opened the door, letting in two young men carrying Mona's heavy steamer trunks.

They stood sheepishly beside Violet waiting for instructions.

"Put the trunks in the dressing room. Violet will show you. Where is Aunt Melanie's luggage?"

Violet offered, "She keeps her luggage in one of the closets in the dressing room."

"Good. Her things should be easy to pack."

"Where should we take her belongings?" Samuel asked.

Mona replied, "To her house, I should think."

Isaac spoke up, "It's not going to be easy to shed Miss Melanie. She's brewing a terrible storm downstairs. Cussing too. Not too ladylike if you ask me."

"Hush, Isaac. Not our place to say," Samuel hissed.

"Take her luggage downstairs and leave it on the front driveway. Tell Jamison to take the luggage to Aunt Melanie's house."

"He's not here," Samuel said.

"Where is he?"

"Jamison took Mr. Deatherage home."

"Of course. Well, leave the luggage in the driveway and tell Jamison to take it over to Aunt Melanie's house when he gets back. That includes my cousins' belongings as well."

Samuel and Isaac glanced at each other before following Violet through the bathroom.

Mona called out, "Violet, bring me one of Aunt Melanie's hatboxes."

Violet dutifully hurried to Mona and handed her a large hatbox.

Mona went through the nightstands, desk, and chests in the room, throwing items into the hatbox. Coming across an address book and a packet of letters, Mona kept them, tucking them in her purse. She also kept a calendar, as well as an old bank statement. After cleaning out the drawers, she checked under the mattress, then the bed, finding nothing but dust bunnies.

Fifteen minutes later, Violet entered the main bedroom and announced, "We are ready, Miss Moon."

"We need to execute this carefully. If I'm correct, my aunt and Mrs. Haggin will be outside the bedroom door waiting for us to open it."

Violet nodded.

"Tell Samuel and Isaac to leave by the maid's door with the luggage once they hear footsteps running down the main staircase. Have them use the same staircase and go out the front door. If my plan goes right, everyone will be scurrying to the back of the house."

"What will I be doing, Miss?"

"You will be explaining through the door to my aunt and Mrs. Haggin that if they don't vacate the second floor, all my aunt's belongings will be thrown from the balcony."

Violet's face drained of color. "I don't know, Miss. Sounds awfully drastic to me."

"It will work. Now let's start."

After Violet gave Samuel and Isaac their instructions, she came back and approached the bedroom door.

Mona gave her an encouraging look.

Violet asked in a quivering voice. "Mrs. Haggin, are you there?"

Two muffled voices sounded as if discussing the question.

"I'm here, Violet. Open this door at once," Mrs. Haggin demanded.

"I'm afraid I can't. I'm to let you know that if you don't go downstairs, Miss Melanie's things will be thrown off the balcony."

"This is outrageous!" Aunt Melanie bellowed, her words slightly slurring. "You better not touch my possessions."

"Sorry, ma'am, but everything has been packed. You're not to cause any trouble. If you do, Miss Moon says your beautiful clothes will be thrown out for you to collect. Please Miss Melanie, don't cause mischief."

Melanie shouted, "How dare you talk to me that way!"

A masculine voice intervened. "Mother, do

come away. You're making a scene. There's a better way to handle this."

Hoping to bluff the women, Violet shouted, "Ma'am, Miss Moon is tossing your luggage over the railing now. Oh my goodness! Everything has dashed out onto the lawn, and the dogs are sniffing about. Hurry before the dogs do their business."

Violet jumped when someone violently kicked the door, but soon heard the clank of the elevator door close, followed by the rattle of cables as the elevator descended to the first floor. She pressed her ear against the door. "I think they're gone, Miss Moon."

"Good. Tell the lads to skedaddle. Luckily our ruse worked and the path is free."

Violet rushed to Samuel and Isaac who jerked the maid's door open and hurried down the front staircase, with their burdens thumping on each stair.

Locking the maid's door, Violet went back into the bedroom where she found Mona watching out the windows.

Seeing Mrs. Haggin and Aunt Melanie rounding the corner, Mona pulled back from the window and sat at the desk. "Well, that's done."

"Oh, Miss, I hope you haven't started something you can't finish. Miss Melanie is awfully strong willed. Only your uncle could control her."

"Thank you for the warning, Violet. Now will you fetch me some hot tea and a couple of sandwiches."

"Surely."

"And leave your key here. Give five taps when you knock, and I'll know it's you."

Violet put the key on the desk and fled. She was pleased Miss Melanie had been thwarted, and her look of anxiety changed to a conspiratorial expression of delight. She didn't know what to make of the new mistress, but knew life would not be dull at Moon Manor.

8

Mona glided down the grand staircase wearing a magnolia printed chiffon dress with butterfly sleeves and a simple gold heart locket her father had given her mother for a wedding gift.

She wasn't sure if she should wear elbow length gloves to dinner, so she carried them in her hand.

At the bottom of the staircase Samuel, dressed in black tails, white tie and gloves, waited for her.

As he helped her down the last several steps, Mona whispered, "Samuel, should I be wearing gloves for dinner? I know if I were in England I might be expected to wear gloves, but I'm not so sure it's the custom here."

Samuel replied, "There is a large brouhaha in the library, Miss. I would suggest that all gloves are off."

Mona smiled. "A bare knuckle fight?"

"Yes, Miss Moon."

"Who's in there?"

"Miss Melanie and Mr. Deatherage. It seems today's escapades have stirred Miss Melanie to the point where she's threatening to have you committed due to insanity."

"Who else is here?"

"Mrs. Deatherage, Mr. Hugh Beaumont, your farm manager, Miss Jetta Dressler, your personal secretary, and your cousins are having cocktails in the front drawing room."

"Hmmm. I guess I better stop the brawling in the library so we may have dinner."

"I would hope so, Miss. The yelling is upsetting the staff and putting the dogs off their feed."

"Thank you, Samuel. Hmm, speaking of dogs, I have Chloe in my room. Tell Violet to walk and feed her. She will also need a bowl of water placed in the bathroom."

"Shall I put her in the kennel for tonight, Miss?"

"No, I'll keep her with me. Did Uncle Manfred put Chloe in the kennel at night?"

"No, Miss, your uncle and Chloe were fast companions. She stayed by his side always. It will be good for her to have a companion again."

"Was Chloe with Uncle Manfred when he passed?"

"Yes, and it made things difficult."

"In what way?"

"Chloe wouldn't let Archer or anyone tend the body, but especially Archer. The vet had to doctor some meat and sedate her before Mr. Manfred could be attended. After that, she was put in the kennel. I have no idea how she got out."

"Hmm."

"Miss. May I escort you to the library?"

"By all means."

Mona followed Samuel down a dark paneled hallway to an ornate door carved with flowers and frolicking naked wood nymphs.

Samuel knocked, opened the door, and announced, "Miss Moon," leaving Mona to face a frustrated Mr. Deatherage and a frazzled, angry Aunt Melanie.

Mona was astonished at how young her aunt was. She knew Melanie had been a mid-life baby, which made her only a few years older. She was quite beautiful with light blonde hair and light eyes, not golden like hers but still unusual and startling. "Good evening," Mona said calmly.

Melanie rose from her chair and screeched, "YOU! How dare you throw me out of the house in which I was born. You're nothing more than an interloper. The daughter of a servant."

"My father lived in this house for twenty-five years. I have every right to be here as its new mistress, as I am the first born of the first born son." She strode over to her aunt and stood before her. "Please Aunt. Let us not quarrel. I've come to make peace."

"Harrumph" Melanie coughed.

Mr. Deatherage, grateful for help in dealing with Melanie, asked, "What do you have in mind, Miss Moon?"

"I'll give my aunt two choices, and she may pick one."

"What could you offer that would make me forget my awful treatment today?" Melanie sneered. She pulled a handkerchief out from one of her banjo sleeves hanging limply from her green taffeta evening gown.

Mona sat in a chair beside her. "I think what I'm about to propose will make the unpleasantness of today a distant memory."

Melanie blew her nose and curiously peeked up at Mona. "Go on."

"I will give you this house and deed it in your name, but I retain my position as head of the family with all my assets intact—both land and monies as stated in Uncle Manfred's will. You will have the prestige of living at Moon Manor again, have your current annual remittance, and I will move to one of the other houses on the estate."

Melanie's eyes brightened.

Mona continued, "But the upkeep of this house and wages for the servants will be taken out of your income—not the estate's general funds."

"I could never afford the upkeep on this house, and you know it."

"Here's my other proposal. I will grant you a one-time disbursement of five thousand dollars, and each of my cousins will receive fifteen hundred dollars if you drop the lawsuit and promise that you and your children will never take legal action against me or the estate ever again. You will welcome me with open arms into this family."

Melanie paused to straighten a bow on her green dress, gaining time to think about the last offer. "Will my annual income remain the same?"

"Yes."

"And my children?"

"Same as before."

"And the five thousand dollars is mine to do with as I please?"

"As long as you don't use it against me or for any nefarious activity. Make up your mind, Auntie. Once we leave this room, all offers are off the table. I'll see you in court, and I have the money to drag this lawsuit out for a very long time."

Mr. Deatherage interjected, "Just a minute, Miss Moon. That's an awful lot of money you're throwing about. The country is still in a Depression you know."

"Can I afford it?"

"That's not the point," Mr. Deatherage begged to differ.

Melanie snapped, "I want ten thousand."

"Six thousand and not a penny more," Mona countered.

"Must be in cash. Under the table. I don't want to pay taxes on it."

Mona looked at Mr. Deatherage who was wiping his forehead with the back of his hand. "You feeling all right, Mr. Deatherage?"

Before he could respond, Melanie blurted, "I'll do it."

A delicious smile appeared on Mona's face. "Good. Mr. Deatherage will write up the terms of the agreement, and as soon as you and my cousins sign the contract, you'll get what's coming to you."

Mr. Deatherage asked, "Which deal are you taking, Melanie? The house or the money?"

Both Mona and Melanie spoke in unison, "THE MONEY, OF COURSE!"

9

Dinner was understandably tense. Mona sat at the head of the table and could feel the seething resentment steaming from her Aunt Melanie and cousins, Meredith and Miles. She would not rest easily until her relatives signed the binding agreement, which would guarantee Mona freedom from any tomfoolery her family might cause in the future. She was going to slip in a clause that if they reneged in any way, Mona would be allowed to lower or disband their annual remittance. Money was the key to controlling her aunt and cousins, and she wanted to hold that power firmly in her hands.

It was not that Mona blamed her relatives' resentment toward her. They had never set eyes on her before this evening, and her father,

Mathias Milton Moon, did cause a great scandal in 1903 by marrying the daughter of the head gardener from Moon Manor. Mona's grandfather swiftly disinherited Mathias when her father refused to walk away from Mona's mother and the two eloped.

The love and admiration Mona felt for her father swelled after seeing all he had surrendered to marry the woman he loved. Forswearing the Moon fortune had been a great sacrifice, and Mona was not sure she would have done the same, but then she had never been in love. She clutched the gold locket around her neck. It contained the pictures of both her parents with the inscription *Forever, MMM.*

Mona's mother had given her the wedding locket shortly before she died of tuberculosis. Mona believed her mother held on to life until she graduated from college. It was the desire to witness Mona walk across the dais and accept her diploma, which had kept her mother going, as not many women graduated from college with honors in 1925, let alone magnum cum laude. A month later, Mona's mother was dead.

As memories rushed through Mona's mind,

she picked at her food and listlessly listened to the conversation around her. She had won the first battle establishing herself as mistress of Moon Manor, but it had taken its toll. She was in desperate need of rest.

"Don't you agree, Mona? MONA!"

Mona looked up. "I'm sorry. What were you saying?"

Willie Deatherage smiled, chirping, "Don't you think it's a good idea?"

"What is?"

"A ball to introduce you to Bluegrass society. Melanie can throw it in your honor."

Mona waved Thomas away as he tried to fill her wine glass. "What are you going on about?"

"Your Aunt Melanie is going to throw a ball in your honor, so you can meet everyone."

"I don't think it's a good idea, Willie."

"It's a great idea," Willie insisted. "How else are you going to meet people?"

Dexter Deatherage interjected, "Now dear, don't bully. If Miss Moon says she doesn't want a ball, then she doesn't want it."

Willie continued, "What's with this Miss Moon jazz? We're in the South. Gentlemen and servants should refer to you as Miss Mona. Miss Moon is too formal, and quit calling my husband Mr. Deatherage. His name is Dexter, or as most people around here pronounce it "Dextah.'"

"Honestly, Willie, you make my head spin," Mona sputtered, not knowing how to respond.

"A ball might be a good idea at that," Dexter contemplated, mulling the idea over. "It would demonstrate the family's support for you. Wouldn't you say, Melanie?"

Melanie threw her napkin on the table, galled at the thought of giving a fancy shindig with Mona as the honored guest, but whined, "I suppose so."

"After all, those papers are not signed yet," Dexter reminded her.

"What papers, Mother?" Miles demanded. "What's old Dexter yammering about?"

"Hush, honey. I'll tell you later."

Meredith insisted, "What is it, Mummy? We have a right to know. Are we staying at Moon Manor after all?"

"Your mother and I have come to an agreement. I'm sure she will inform you both later," Mona said.

"I want to know now," Miles said, his body stiffening with tension.

"Oh, be quiet. Both of you. Let me handle this," Melanie snapped.

"I'd be happy to help. I think it sounds dreamy," Jetta Dressler said.

"That's the spirit," Willie said, waving to the butler for more wine.

Mona studied her social secretary, Miss Jetta, whom she had inherited along with Moon Manor. It was the first time Mona really paid attention to her.

Miss Jetta wore a plain velvet gown that was out of style, but she was immaculately groomed and tidy. Her long hair was braided and wrapped around her head in a golden brown halo. While it was attractive, it was very old fashioned and hard to take care of, so Mona wondered why Jetta didn't get her hair cut in some of the shorter hairstyles women were currently sporting.

"Are you sure the three of you can pull this off?" Dexter asked.

"Oh, I just came up with the idea. I'm not actually helping. Maybe supervising a little here and there," Willie said before taking a sip of wine.

Hugh Beaumont said, "I can help also, mainly with getting valets for the automobiles, making sure the grounds are spotless, that sort of thing. We all certainly want to put our best foot forward for Miss Mona." He smiled warmly at Mona, which was not lost on Melanie.

"That's very sweet of you, Hugh," Melanie barked.

"It's important that Miss Mona's transition to head of the Moon fortune be made as seamless as possible. Do you know much about the Moon business, Miss Mona?" Hugh asked, ignoring Melanie's sharp tone.

Mona wondered if there was something between them. She would have sworn Melanie and Hugh were playing some sort of *tiddlywinks* under the table during dinner. Mona repressed the urge to bend under the table and peek. Yet, now Hugh was doing his utmost to capture Mona's attention by gazing intently at her when he spoke.

She gave Hugh Beaumont a quick study. Like Dexter and Miles, he was wearing a black dinner jacket with square shoulders and a black bow tie with a starched white shirt and black waistcoat. Hugh wasn't handsome but sexy in an ugly kind of way with his penciled thin mustache and sharp cheekbones. For a working Joe, he had very expressive hands. His fingers were long and elegant with nails recently manicured. He was a man whom women noticed. Catching Mona's perusal of him, he boldly stared back until Jetta asked him to pass the salt.

Mona was relieved the stare down had been interrupted. She gave a quick smile at Jetta whom she thought had come to her rescue on purpose. Sharp cookie there.

"What I don't know, I'll learn," Mona assured.

Meredith asked, "May I attend the ball, Mother?"

"You haven't been presented to society yet."

"I have no problem with Meredith coming," Mona assured.

"I'd liked to be called Mimi, if you please. I've never liked the name Meredith."

"All right, Mimi. I'll remember in the future," Mona shot back, thinking Mimi dressed a little older than she should. No doubt she was a mature-looking young lady for her age, but Mimi's perpetual expression of entitled smugness made her seem unattractive.

With a prim look on her face, Mimi turned once again to her mother. "May I come? Mona said it was fine with her."

"It's Miss Mona for you and no. You must wait until you've been presented as a debutante."

Mimi threw her napkin on the table and crossing her arms, shot her mother a petulant look. "I never get to do anything."

Mona tried to ease the tension at the table. "Mimi, have you decided upon a college? Perhaps Transylvania University like your brother?"

"College? Why would I want to go to college when I'm to marry a rich man?" She sneered at her mother. "But I need to come out in society in order to meet men."

"Your time will come very soon. I promise. Now honey, don't be cross." Melanie turned to the butler. "Thomas, what do we have for dessert?"

"Miss Mimi's favorite—orange cake with a white coconut frosting."

"See there, honey. Just for you."

Mona placed her napkin to the left of her plate. "It's been a long day. I'll think I'll retire."

The three men stood.

"No please, stay and enjoy your dessert." Giving a slight nod to her secretary, Mona said, "Miss Jetta, I'll see you in the morning."

"I hope your plans include me tomorrow," Hugh drawled, giving Mona a languid glance.

Ignoring him, Mona asked Dexter, "May I see you for a moment?"

"Surely. Willie, darling, I'll be just a moment. Don't eat my cake now."

"As if I would," Willie cooed, watching Thomas slice delicious slabs of gâteau à l'orange.

Dexter followed Mona into the hallway.

Mona whispered, "Dexter, I know you're tired, but can you stay and make sure all my guests leave the house? I don't trust Melanie to leave of her own accord."

"Thomas will see to it."

"He doesn't have the authority to make them leave, but you do. Besides he's known Melanie and those kids all his life. He's not going to side with me."

"He's not going to jeopardize his job either, but I'll hang about if that's what you want."

"Better yet, why don't you and Willie stay tonight?"

Dexter thought for a moment. "I will stay

long enough to make sure everyone is gone and all windows and doors are locked up tight, but I want to sleep in my own bed."

Mona exhaled built-up tension. "I apologize, Dexter. I'm taking up way too much of your time. You and Willie were so kind to attend dinner tonight. Please forgive me."

"I don't see why you're so jumpy. You've been in rougher places than this, besides you have your revolver."

"It's just that from the time I set foot in this house, I felt a sudden sense of foreboding. I can't explain it, but there it is. Silly I know."

"I think what you need is a good night's sleep. You've won the first battle, and maybe even the war. There's nothing to worry about. Things will look better in the morning."

"Perhaps you're right. Well, goodnight then. I'll see you tomorrow morning."

"Make that late tomorrow afternoon. I want to spend some time with my wife."

Catching Dexter's meaning, Mona smiled as she headed up the staircase, but she just couldn't shake the awful feeling the next shoe was going to drop.

And Mona always trusted her gut.

10

"Miss, is there something you need to tell me? No one has ever locked a bedroom door in Moon Manor, let alone the front door of the house."

"I know you think this over the top, but I have my reasons, Violet."

Violet nodded but looked worried.

Seeing Violet's concern, Mona knew if she was ever to gain this young woman's trust, she had to be honest. "Violet, when I was in India, a rich man died and left his estate to a distant relative. The relative accepted the inheritance and came to live in the dead man's house. Within two weeks, another relative who thought he should have received the estate murdered the heir. Emotions are running high, and I don't know anyone here—not so that I could trust them. I'd rather be safe than sorry. At least until I get my bearings. I hope you understand."

"Yes, but people in India are not Christians."

Mona smiled at the naiveté of Violet's statement. "Actually, the family in question was British, and the murderer was an Anglican reverend—a nephew of the deceased who stabbed the unlucky heir to death in his sleep. So you see, when a great deal of money is involved, people lose perspective."

"Yes, Miss. I'm sorry if I overstepped."

"Quite all right, Violet. By the way, were you my aunt's maid?"

"No one's, Miss. I've never been a lady's maid before."

"What were you then?"

"A maid of all work, but I have taken some courses through the mail, and Thomas gave me tips."

"Do you want to be a lady's maid?"

"I'm a good worker, and I need work that pays the best."

"How much is your pay?"

"One hundred and twenty-five dollars a year."

Mona was surprised. She knew personal maids made two hundred fifty dollars in the North plus keep. "Do you live on Mooncrest Farm?"

"My mother has a small house on the estate, but I moved into Moon Manor when I was chosen."

"Does the rest of the staff live in Moon Manor also?"

"Mrs. Haggin and Miss Jetta live on the third floor and Thomas and Samuel have rooms in the male servants' quarters in the basement. The rest of the staff go to their homes after dinner is served."

"Who decided you would be my maid?"

"Miss Jetta."

"Not Mrs. Haggin?"

"There was a great deal of discussion between Miss Jetta and Mrs. Haggin about it. Mrs. Haggin wanted Dora as she is the senior housemaid, but she didn't have any training in waitin' on a lady. Finally, Mr. Deatherage stepped in and decided I should take the position, mainly because I'm handy with a needle and thread."

"Are you making more money now than before?"

"Yes."

"And I provide your uniforms, meals, and lodging as part of your stipend?"

"Yes, Miss."

"What days do you get off?"

"I get Thursday afternoons and Sunday evenings off."

"What are your hours?"

"My hours? I'm not sure what you mean. I'm on call from sunrise until you go to bed. Whenever you need me, except for my official time off."

"I see I have a lot to learn about managing a manor house and a horse farm, let alone copper mines."

"No need to worry yourself about it, Miss Mona. You got men folks to do that for you."

"One thing I've learned is not to depend on other people, especially men. They like to take advantage of women, especially single females."

"Not Mr. Deatherage. He was Mr. Moon's right hand man. You can trust him."

"We'll see. Let's change the subject. Is there a personal relationship between my Aunt Melanie and Hugh Beaumont? I noticed a type of tension between them at dinner."

"Mr. Beaumont is Miss Melanie's particular friend."

"But nothing official?"

"No, Miss, but everyone knows, except Miss Melanie doesn't know that everyone knows."

"Don't Miss Melanie's friends approve?"

"Mr. Beaumont has a reputation, if you know what I mean, but he is the scion of an old family who has lost their money. He is still welcomed at social events, but mothers keep an eye on their daughters, if you know what I mean. Besides, he's an employee. He's not Miss Melanie's equal. Not anymore."

"I won't mention our little talk, Violet. I know you must be tired, so go to bed."

"Don't you need help undressing?"

"I would rather dress and undress myself in private. You take care of the suite, my clothes, and run errands for me."

Violet frowned. "Folks will think badly of me if I don't help with dressing you. They will think I'm lazy. Have I done something to offend you?"

Mona knew from previous experience servants can be very touchy about perceived insults.

"Well, if you don't tell anyone, and I don't, who's to know? It will be our little secret."

"Like Miss Melanie's secret?"

"No. A real secret."

Seeing Violet was not reassured, Mona added, "I'm feeling my way through this adventure. Right now, I need to feel safe and have some time to acclimate to my new position as heiress. I'm counting on you to help me with this transition. However, if you are not happy, we can find another position for you."

"You *was* counting on me?"

Mona noticed Violet used words like scion, but then used wrong verb tenses at times. She wondered what was behind it. "Yes, I need you to help by being a buffer. As I explained before, I don't want anyone in this suite but you and me. Keep the rooms clean. Keep my clothes in good order, and if you hear something of which I should be informed, let me know."

"You mean more secrets?"

"Think of yourself as my eyes and ears when I'm not around."

Violet brightened. "I can do that. People blab all the time around me. They just forget I'm there. I hear lots of stuff. Lots."

"Good. We'll start tomorrow working things out. Right now I'm exhausted. Run along to bed, Violet."

"Yes, Miss. Shall I put Chloe out?"

"No, Chloe will stay with me. I like having her around."

"Goodnight, Miss." Violet marched to her room, leaving Mona to throw off her evening gown, neatly hanging it over a chair. She donned a lavender silk negligee she had bought in Cincinnati. As a precaution, Mona wedged chairs against the doors leading from her bedroom, even the door that led to the maid's room.

It wasn't that Mona didn't want to trust Violet. It was just that Mona didn't trust Violet. Not yet, anyway.

11

In the middle of the night, Mona awoke to the sound of Chloe softly growling, alerting Mona to someone inserting a key into the lock and gently twisting the knob of her door. Pushing silently, the perpetrator found the door stubbornly held.

Mona lightly tiptoed over and put her ear against the wall. The intruder vainly tried to open the door again, but the chair jammed against the door remained steadfast.

The full moon was bright and provided ample light through the windows. Retrieving her revolver, Mona took careful aim and squeezed the trigger, shooting through the top of the wooden door.

Mona shouted above Chloe's fierce barking. "If you try to get in my room again, the next shot will be lower!" She heard the intruder scurry down the staircase. Grabbing the skeleton key, Mona pulled the chair away, and unlocking the door, she and Chloe gave chase.

The front door stood wide open. Grasping Chloe's collar, Mona stepped out onto the portico flanked by the imposing lions, which cast eerie shadows in the cold light of the moon. Seeing no movement, she knew the intruder had successfully fled the scene. Most probably, the trespasser had run behind the house, and Mona was not going to give chase in her bare feet. She knew better than to plunge headlong into a possible trap.

Thomas and Samuel ran up behind Mona, breathing heavily.

"What's happened?" Thomas asked. He and Samuel tried not to show surprise at seeing their employer dressed in a thin negligee, brandishing a gun with one hand and holding on to a snarling, excited poodle with the other.

"We heard a gunshot," Samuel said.

"It's over."

Thomas gave Mona a strange look while holding the front door open as Mona and Chloe stepped back through and started upstairs.

Turning on the staircase Mona asked, "Thomas, you did lock all the doors after our guests left?"

"Mr. Miles is still here. He was too under the weather to go home, so he stayed on, but I did lock all the doors after everyone else left."

Mona sighed. "You mean he was drunk. Who gave him leave to stay?"

"Mr. Deatherage," Thomas answered.

"Samuel, see if Miles is in his room. Thomas, recheck all the doors and windows to make sure they're locked."

"Yes, Miss. What should I do if Mr. Miles is not to be located?" Samuel asked.

"Nothing at the moment. We'll sort it out later. One more thing, Thomas."

"Yes, Miss?"

"It seems there's been a little damage to my bedroom door. See that it is fixed, please."

Both Thomas and Samuel shot each other a curious glance.

Mona ascended the staircase with Chloe. "Goodnight, gentlemen."

Thomas and Samuel sang in chorus, "Goodnight, Miss Mona."

Mona had one last chore to do before she went back to bed. She turned on the upstairs hall light and unlocked the door to the maid's room. There slept Violet snoring lightly. Mona could tell by Violet's body contour and her slack jaw that Violet was really in lala land and not pretending. "Well, I know Violet's a heavy sleeper now," Mona muttered.

She eased the door shut and locked it. Believing the night's events were over, Mona went back to her room, but not before Chloe jumped into the big four-poster bed.

Mona didn't push her away. To tell the truth, Mona didn't mind the company and was determined for Chloe to become her good friend. Mona desperately needed a pal at Moon Manor—even if it was only a dog.

12

Mona awoke to five light taps on the door and a key turning in the lock. Seeing her precaution of a chair against the door had fallen away, Mona instinctively grabbed her gun and aimed at the door.

The door opened and in strode Violet carrying a tray laden with food. Upon seeing a gun pointed at her, Violet nearly dropped the tray.

"Oh, it's you."

"Yes, Miss Mona. I've brought your breakfast."

"What time is it?"

"Nine. It's late I know, but apparently there was an upset last night."

"What about?"

"I don't know, but there is a lot of whispering

in the kitchen."

Violet laid the tray on the bed. "I'll draw your bath."

"Don't bother, Violet. I'll take a quick shower. Please lay out an outfit for this morning. You know best about these matters."

"You have a nice day frock, which will be suitable as it's going to be warm today. If you don't mind me saying so, Miss Mona, you need more clothes. I used to mend Miss Melanie's things when she lived here, and I know from her wardrobe that you don't have enough outfits for a lady of your position."

"When did my aunt last reside here?"

"Up to a year or so ago. She and the children lived here with Mr. Moon until he ordered her out of the house."

"Why?"

"Don't know, but they had a row about something," Violet said, picking up Mona's clothes left on the chair and desk.

"Violet, the door."

"Oh, I forgot. Sorry, Miss," Violet said, rushing to the door and locking it. As she removed the key from the lock, the splintered cavity at the top of the door caught her attention. "Miss, the door's been damaged. There's a hole at the top."

"Yes, I know. I put it there."

Violet spun around with a surprised expression on her face.

Mona studied the breakfast tray. "Violet, can you tell me what all this is?"

"Mrs. Haggin didn't know what you liked, so she had the cook put everything on your tray. It's a complete Southern breakfast. You got two eggs sunny side up, fried country ham with red-eye gravy, biscuits with country gravy on the side, grits, hoecakes, coffee, and orange juice."

"I'm surprised you could carry this heavy tray up the steps."

"I'm young and strong."

"Well, thank you."

"You best hurry. Miss Jetta and Mr. Beaumont are having their breakfast downstairs."

"Do they always have breakfast here?"

"Yes, Miss Mona, the cook always lays out a buffet breakfast in the breakfast dining room."

"There's more than one dining room?"

Violet gave Mona a look of despair, thinking this Yankee woman didn't know anything and took care to explain. "Moon Manor has three official dining rooms. There's the formal dining room where dinner is served, the informal dining room where breakfast and lunch are served, and the downstairs dining hall where the servants eat."

Mona smiled and noting Violet's frustration, said, "Thank you. Please give the cook instructions that I will take my breakfast in the informal dining room until further notice, and I promise to purchase more outfits as not to shame you, Violet."

Violet was pleased and took Mona's evening clothes into the dressing room.

Alone at last, Mona ate with relish, as she had not eaten much yesterday and was famished. She tried everything. She ate the eggs and biscuits with gusto. Only when she got to the last biscuit did she spoon country gravy on it. To Mona's surprise, she enjoyed it. Growing a bit more adventurous, she took a bite of the country ham. Hmm, too salty for her taste. Now for the grits. Oh yes, she loved the pat of butter melted into the creamy center of the grits.

Thoroughly stuffed, Mona put the tray aside, climbed out of bed, and made ready for her first full day as mistress at Moon Manor.

13

As Mona was conferring with Jetta in the library about the upcoming ball, Mrs. Haggin rushed in. "Miss Mona, I don't understand what's happening!"

Mona answered, "It's very simple. The locks are being changed."

"But why?"

"That's not for you to question. The locks of my bedroom suite and all the outside doors are being refitted."

"Very well. I'll make sure all the keys are labeled."

"I'm sorry, Mrs. Haggin, but the locksmith has orders to turn the keys over to me, and only me."

A crimson flush ran up Mrs. Haggin's neck

and face as she clasped her hands together in a tight ball.

"This is in no way a reflection on you, but there is a third key to my suite which someone used to try to break into my room last night."

Mrs. Haggin wheezed in obvious distress. "Miss Mona, I swear there are only two keys to the master suite. I have never known the existence of a third key."

"There's another matter. I gave explicit instructions that no one outside the staff was to spend the night at Moon Manor, but I find Cousin Miles was allowed to stay. Why was that?"

Mrs. Haggin sniffed. "I wouldn't know. As my duties were finished, I went to bed around ten. You'll have to inquire elsewhere. Is that all, Miss?"

Mona believed it was time to sprinkle a little sugar. She needed Mrs. Haggin on her side. If she couldn't achieve friendship, she needn't make an enemy of the woman either. "One more thing. Mrs. Haggin, I have been told you were a loyal and devoted employee to Uncle Manfred."

"He was a good man."

"I know this is a difficult adjustment for the

staff, but in time things will settle down and resume a routine again. Just be patient, Mrs. Haggin. I'm counting on you for help in this matter. Except for a few minor changes, your responsibilities will remain consistent as they were under Uncle Manfred."

Mrs. Haggin's demeanor brightened. "I will assist as best I can."

"Very well. I want to inspect the house after lunch."

"It would be my pleasure." Mrs. Haggin smiled as she was proud of Moon Manor and would enjoy giving the new owner a tour. "Are there any other instructions?"

"No, thank you. You may go."

Leaving the library, Mrs. Haggin quietly closed the door behind her.

"That was very sweet of you to ask Mrs. Haggin for help. Makes her feel useful," Jetta remarked, placing files on a massive carved desk. "You get more with honey than with vinegar like we say in the South."

Mona opened a file. "I'm not so sure. Vinegar can be a very useful tool. Its acid can remove noxious things."

Jetta frowned for a second before hiding her disapproval. She couldn't be critical of Mona Moon, needing her job as she did.

"What am I looking at?" Mona asked, peering down a long list of names.

"These are the invitees to the ball. Do they meet with your approval?"

"I have no idea who they are, so invite whom you please."

"Miss Mona, you should take this ball very seriously. The men who own these horse farms are important in the fields of commerce and politics. Most of them only visit the Bluegrass during racing season, but they will come to the ball in order to meet you. You are only one of a few women who own a Thoroughbred farm, and it's the largest one in the world. Only Edward Bradley who owns Idle Hour Stock Farm can challenge you in terms of acreage and prestige."

"Who is Edward Bradley?"

"He's an older gent, but he has all his teeth and can bite, if you get my meaning."

"Does he have a horse in the Kentucky Derby?"

"A dud by the name of Brokers Tip, which

has never won a race, but don't kid yourself by that. Mr. Edwards has won the Kentucky Derby in 1921, 1926, and 1932. Also the Preakness in 1917 and 1932, not to mention the Belmont in 1929."

"Goodness."

"He made his fortune by gambling. He's no one to trifle with, Miss Mona. He served as a scout for General Miles during the Indian War campaigns and was a friend of Wyatt Earp."

"With all this new money buying up the horse farms, are there any original owners still left?"

"A few like the Keene family, but times are hard and many had to sell. I know I shouldn't say this, but people's livelihoods depend on you making a good impression. You may be rich as Midas, but these guests can cause a lot of grief if they don't cotton to you."

Realizing a great deal was at stake, Mona patted her secretary's hand. "Don't fret, Jetta. I'll do my duty and make you proud. Now tell me everything I need to know about the people on this list. If you have photographs, it would be a great help."

Jetta pulled up a chair, tucking back wisps of

hair dangling in her freckled face, and began schooling Mona Moon about the *who's who* in the rarified world of Thoroughbred racing.

14

"What on earth are you doing?" Dexter asked, strolling into the library.

Mona peered over a stack of magazines and photo albums she was studying. "I am placing faces with names from the guest list. My secretary has turned this ball into a study course worthy of an ivy-league university."

"Good idea. Nothing like learning the enemies' weaknesses before battle."

"Why do you assume they are enemies?"

"Not only are you a woman, but you're not one of them." Dexter paused. "Oh dear, I've really stuck my foot in my mouth this time."

"I know what you mean, and it will be an uphill battle, but I have a plan to conquer the Huns."

"How?"

"Can't tell you. You might blab to Willie who will blab to everyone else."

Dexter grabbed at his heart. "You cut me to the quick with your cynicism."

Mona laughed.

"I understand because I do tell Wilhelmina everything that isn't under client-lawyer privilege, which is sacred to me."

"Dexter, everything you and I say to one another is privileged."

"Oh."

"Tell Willie if she wants Moon Manor gossip, she must come to the source."

"I hear and I obey." Dexter clicked his heels together and gave a stiff bow.

"I see your briefcase is bulging. Let me move some of this material out of your way." Mona picked up stacks of photo albums and magazines, placing them in a chair. "Before we start, Dexter, I want to ask you something."

"Go ahead," Dexter replied, pulling a sheaf of papers from his briefcase.

"I inspected the house after lunch, and quite frankly, I'm appalled at its condition."

"Yes, that."

"The house is so dark and gloomy, not to mention the kitchen needs upgrading—only one tiny refrigerator for this big house. The pantry is disorganized and not properly lit. I don't know how the cook manages. The servants' quarters haven't seen paint since Grover Cleveland was President, and the bathroom downstairs is underwhelming, not to mention there is no proper bathroom on the third floor. Did you know the laundress is still doing the wash by hand? We need a new washer with a wringer on the top, plus the furniture in this mausoleum is Victorian and out of date. Even the bed linen is old and frayed. Can't we postpone this fête until I can get things in order?"

"No can do. Invitations were sent out yesterday. It's already the talk of the town. Three chaps from my club called the house to ask me about it, and Willie has made an appointment with her dressmaker. You are giving a party the night before the Kentucky Derby. It's all set. You can't back out now."

Mona leaned back in her chair, twisting her mouth in frustration. "I see. Well, if the invitations have gone out, there's nothing more to be said. What's done is done. I was hoping to have more time."

"The party will be at night. Using candles and putting the electric lights low will hide a multitude of sins."

"How did things at Moon Manor become so tattered?"

"The farm itself is in tiptop shape. It's where Manfred spent most of the money. I don't think he cared for change at Moon Manor and let things slide."

"Maybe I should go live in the stables."

"I was hoping you would address this matter."

"What are you handing me?"

"It is an up-to-date spreadsheet of all your assets and liabilities. Also included is a budget for repairs and upgrades to the house. We'll have no trouble getting the best people."

Mona perused the documents. "You're a man after my own heart." She looked up from the papers. "Willie made you do this?"

"Yep. You caught me."

"I assume you have a list of recommended workmen."

"Anybody in this town with a hammer will want to claim the bragging rights that they worked on this house."

Mona flapped the papers at Dexter. "I will look this over and get back to you. You know I took accounting courses in college."

"Didn't realize."

"I have one more thing to ask. I can't find Uncle Manfred's death certificate anywhere. Do you have a copy?"

"Why would you want to see his death certificate?"

Mona ignored Dexter's question. "Do you have the official copy?"

Dexter reached inside his briefcase and pulled out a typed and embossed certificate, handing it to Mona.

While Mona glanced over the certificate, she asked, "Did you know Miles stayed over last night?"

"Yes, I let him."

"Why?"

"He was blind drunk. I thought it best. The servants were to whisk him away before you awoke. Is he still here?"

"Don't know, but I do know someone tried to break into my bedroom. That's why I wanted all the Moons out of the house last night."

Dexter was flabbergasted. "But how? You have the only keys."

"There must be a third key."

"What happened?"

"I shot at the perpetrator and chased him out of the house?"

"Was it Miles?"

"Samuel was to check to see if Miles was still in his room?"

"And?"

"I haven't spoken to him yet."

"Let's straighten this out now." Dexter rang the servants' cord.

They waited quietly until Samuel entered the room.

"You rang, Miss?"

Dexter asked, "Samuel, after the incident last night, was Mr. Miles in his room?"

"No sir. The bed was disturbed, but Mr. Miles was absent."

"Do you know where he is now?" Mona asked.

"I took the liberty of phoning your aunt's house. Archer told me Mr. Miles stumbled home drunk around two this morning. Those were Archer's words, Miss, not mine."

Mona thanked Samuel and gave him leave to go.

Dexter apologized. "I'm sorry, Mona. If I had any idea that Miles would be up to mischief, I wouldn't have let him stay, but he could hardly stand."

"It was near three when I chased someone out of the house. Would Archer lie about the time for Miles?"

"Why should he?"

"Why does anyone do anything? Sex, money, or power, or a combination of the three."

"You're very cynical for a young woman."

"Had to be. School of hard knocks. I don't know if you've noticed this, Dexter, but it's rough out there, especially for women and children. Please follow my instructions to the letter next time."

Dexter nodded, duly chastised. He had put his client in danger.

Mona put the death certificate in one of the

desk's drawers and locked it. "It's about time for tea. Would you like to stay?"

"I could do with a cup of coffee. I'm starting to drag a little."

"Then let's retire to the parlor."

"I could fancy a sandwich, too."

"Yes, quite," Mona answered, wondering why Dexter had seemed so hesitant to give her Uncle Manfred's death certificate. As soon as she got a chance, she was going to study it.

When she had asked the staff about Uncle Manfred, they said he was a good employer, and she should ask Mr. Deatherage for any information. They seemed nervous with her questions.

Mona was determined to find out why because nothing about the inheritance felt right to her.

Nothing at all.

15

It was late before Mona was able to get back to her paperwork before going to bed. There was tea, an emergency with an employee getting kicked by an unruly stallion, and finally, dinner with Jetta and Hugh Beaumont who reported on the employee's condition.

Mona made sure Hugh understood Mooncrest Farm would pay for the employee's hospital bills, and his family would still receive pay during the man's convalescence.

Hugh argued paying the hospital bills would only encourage laziness and negligence among the workers.

Mona politely listened to Hugh's concerns while she dove into a baked peach cobbler a la mode. "I think I've made my wishes clear. I'll

MURDER UNDER A BLUE MOON

have Mr. Deatherage handle it. Thank you."

Mona, Jetta, and Hugh finished their dessert in silence until Mona spoke, "Thomas, thank Monsieur Bisaillon for a delicious meal."

"Yes, Miss Mona," Thomas replied, happy the meal service had gone off without a flaw. Stuffed celery with cream cheese as an appetizer, petite filet de boeuf with buttered garden peas and honeyed carrots, raw julienne cabbage with a sweet balsamic dressing for a salad, and hot buttered rolls.

"If you all will excuse me, I'm very tired," Mona said as the butler pulled out her chair and picked up her napkin, which had fallen to the floor.

Jetta chimed, "Goodnight, Miss Mona."

"Yes, goodnight, Jetta. Mr. Beaumont."

"Goodnight, Miss," Hugh murmured, winking at her.

Mona quickly escaped to the library where she collected the accounting files and Uncle Manfred's death certificate. She wanted only to undress, snuggle under the covers with Chloe, and listen to comedian Jack Benny on the radio while going over her papers.

When she unlocked her bedroom door, Violet was waiting for her with a freshly laundered negligee, robe, and slippers.

Mona did not grumble as Violet helped her out of the complicated evening gown. "Did you have a nice afternoon, Violet?"

"Yes, Miss Mona. After I tidied up the suite, I went to help my mother."

"Doing what?"

"She's cooking for the Boller family and taking meals over to their house."

"Is it Mr. Boller who's suffering from a horse kick?"

"Yes, Miss Mona. He was struck in the head as he was grooming the horse."

"I should go and see him in the hospital. Tell your mother to hand over the receipts, and I'll reimburse her."

"Everything she cooks is from the farm—chickens, collard greens, potatoes, eggs."

"Didn't realize. I need to take a tour of the estate."

"Let Mr. Gallo take you. No one knows this place better than Mr. Gallo."

"Point well taken. Can we take this up in the

morning, Violet?"

"Yes, Miss." Violet seemed hesitant to leave.

"What is it?"

"I was wondering if I could go into town to see a late movie. The Ben Ali Theater is showing the new Joan Crawford film."

Waving her hand dismissively, Mona spouted, "Yes, just don't forget to lock up when you come back."

"Thank you, Miss." Giddy, Violet flew out of the room. She had to get Miss Mona's clothes laid out for the next day, change, and meet her girlfriend at the movie palace in less than forty-five minutes. Maybe she could get Jamison to drive her into town if she paid him a nickel. It was worth a try.

Hearing an exuberant Violet getting ready, Mona gave a wisp of a smile. She remembered being eighteen and excited at what the world had to offer. Seemed like such a long time ago.

Mona concentrated on the death certificate in front of her. Official cause of death was heart stoppage exacerbated by pneumonia. Mona bit her lip. Manfred Moon was a middle-aged gentleman, so a heart attack was not out of the question, but the notes at the bottom of the death certificate startled Mona. It stated that Manfred Michael Moon had sustained two broken ribs, one cracked rib, and a severe gash on the side of his head. No explanation of those injuries.

Obviously, there had been some sort of accident leading to her uncle's demise. She started to ring for Violet. Oh goodness. Violet had gone into town by now.

Mona laid her gun on the nightstand and slid deeper under the covers, turning off the light. Tomorrow, she would ask the servants. They would know what happened to Manfred Moon.

The question was would they be willing to speak?

16

"Thomas, were you here during my uncle's last days?" Mona asked, catching him in the butler's pantry.

Thomas jumped a bit, as he was not used to his employer sneaking up on him in the servants' domain. "Yes'am. I'm always here," he replied, looking a bit confused. Where else would he be?

"Can you tell me a little bit about his death?"

He thought for a moment and looked around to see if anyone was listening. "Well, he was getting on in years, and was not as spry as he used to be, but it seemed like he went downhill sudden like. There was a vicious cold snap in January, and he caught the flu, but he was getting better. Even came downstairs for dinner now and then. He was on the mend, and then he came down with pneumonia. You know how that takes down folks quickly. His lungs kept filling up, and that was that."

"The death certificate said heart stoppage exacerbated by pneumonia."

"I was in the room when Mr. Moon was pronounced dead. That's what the doctor said to Mr. Deatherage as cause of death."

"Mr. Deatherage was present when my uncle died?"

"Yes'am. Mr. Deatherage was here quite often during those last months. Mr. Moon was having him do lots of changes."

"What kind of changes?"

"I wouldn't know, but I would guess one of them was making you the new heir."

"You mean I wasn't intended to be the heir originally?"

"Miss, I'm just guessing, but I do know when Mr. Deatherage told Miss Melanie she was no longer the heir, all hell broke loose, if you don't mind my saying so." Thomas looked at the silver on the shelves. "Miss, these are matters better taken up with Mr. Deatherage. This is polishing day, and I've got to start now or we won't get done in time for dinner."

Mona could tell the butler was uncomfortable speaking about her uncle's death. "One more thing. There were notes on the certificate, which stated Uncle Manfred had broken and cracked ribs. How could a bedridden man get broken ribs?"

"He fell down the stairs, Miss. A terrible accident, it was."

"How did it happen?"

"I guess he got confused and fell."

"Wasn't there a nurse with him?"

"She said she fell asleep."

"Who found him?"

"Samuel and I found Archer standing over Mr. Moon. I guess he had been up as he was dressed. We helped carry Mr. Moon to his room, and the nurse called the doctor."

"If my uncle had wanted something, why didn't he ring for someone? Didn't Archer sleep in the small room off the master suite?"

"Yes, Miss."

"Anything else different that night?"

"Mr. Moon mentioned he hoped dinner wouldn't give him heartburn. He felt it too spicy and ordered beef broth for the next day. Another thing, the lights in the hallways and staircase were turned off. We had been keeping them on for the nurse in case she had to make a trip to the kitchen."

"Was it usual for the nurse to fall asleep?"

"She was the night nurse. I always found her to be conscientious and was surprised to find her sleeping on the job. When I tried to wake her, she seemed groggy."

"If your quarters are in the basement, how do you know things, Thomas? How did you hear the commotion at my bedroom door the other evening? How did you know Uncle Manfred fell?"

Thomas grinned. "The heat registers. Sound gets sucked through the ducts to the basement, and if someone uses the bathrooms on the second and third floors, the pipes rattle. Like listening to the radio. Is that all, Miss Mona?"

Mona felt her cheeks grow hot. The male servants, who had their quarters in the basement, knew her every move, especially at night. She wondered if the female servants on the third floor heard the same. There was no privacy in this huge mansion. "Thank you, Thomas."

"Yes'am."

Mrs. Haggin strode into the pantry and stopped abruptly at the sight of seeing Mona speaking with Thomas.

Thomas quickly lifted a tray filled with silverware and scurried into the kitchen.

"May I help you, Miss Mona?"

"Can you get me a torch please?"

"A torch?"

Mona chuckled. "I'm sorry. I lived in London for a year. They call it a torch."

Mrs. Haggin still looked confused.

"I need a flashlight."

Mrs. Haggin opened a drawer and pulled one out. "Will that be all?"

"Would you put a dozen flashlights on the shopping list, Mrs. Haggin?"

"If you wish."

"Then give them to me."

"All twelve?"

"Yes, and buy plenty of batteries for them, too."

"I shall make sure we procure them today."

"Thank you. That is all, Mrs. Haggin."

"Very good, Miss," she said before she turned to venture into the kitchen. She knew Mona was watching her. Mrs. Haggin didn't mind being dismissed, as she wanted to ask Thomas what he and the mistress had been whispering about in the butler's pantry. She thought she had heard something about Manfred Moon's death.

Mrs. Haggin was concerned about the new mistress of Moon Manor. In many ways, Miss Mona was a most attentive employer. She didn't make outrageous demands like some masters on surrounding farms. She never fussed about the menus and ate whatever was placed in front of her. She even hired extra workers to clean Moon Mansion for the ball, which lessened Mrs. Haggin's workload considerably, not to mention that of Dora and Mabelle. And best of all, employees who worked on the estate received a raise of fifty-cents up to a dollar per week, depending on their status. All the servants had been taken by surprise by Mona's generosity.

Manfred Moon never believed in *spoiling* the house servants and farm workers, and of course, very few employers even considered giving a raise during the Depression, so Miss Mona was looked upon with favor by the staff—at least for now.

Mrs. Haggin thought she had been too critical of Mona when she first alighted from the Daimler. She was a Yankee, and her father had been disowned by the family, but Miss Mona was proving to be a good mistress.

So, perhaps she would give Mona Moon the benefit of doubt. Maybe. She was still stewing on it.

17

Violet leaned over the second floor banister and called, "Miss Mona, Thomas wants me to tell you that your breakfast is getting cold."

"Uhuh," Mona mumbled, sitting on the top step of the staircase feeling along the baseboard with a flashlight protruding from her mouth.

"What you're doing is dangerous. You could slip, and the flashlight would chip your beautiful teeth. It would be a shame to mar them."

Mona scooted down another step and felt along the wall, baseboard, and the banister. "Violet, come here and sit beside me." Mona made room for her.

"What am I supposed to be doing?"

"I want you to close your eyes and feel along the wall."

"Any particular reason, Miss?"

"Just use your fingers and explore. Let me know if you feel something unusual."

Violet did as bidden and slowly felt the wall-paper and then the wood of the baseboard. "It's not smooth right here."

"You feel it, too!" Mona said excitedly. She pulled a magnifying glass from her wide-legged lounging pajamas and bent over to where Violet was still rubbing with her fingers.

"Move your hand, Violet," Mona ordered, while gazing at the spot with the magnifying glass. "I see it. I see it!"

"What, Miss?" Violet asked, caught up in the excitement.

Mona handed Violet the magnifying glass. "Tell me what you see."

Violet bent over and caught the imperfection with her fingers again. She had never used a magnifying glass before and it took her several seconds to focus on the image. "Looks like a tiny hole in the wall."

"It does, doesn't it! If I'm correct, there should be a similar hole on the banister directly across from it. Yes, yes. I found it. There's another small hole corresponding to the hole on the baseboard."

"What does it mean, Miss Mona?"

"It means murder, Violet. Murder most foul!"

18

After weeks of preparation, the night of the grand ball arrived. The house sparkled from a thousand beeswax candles placed in all the windows and every room of the house. Their pleasing aroma combined with dozens of sweet smelling flower arrangements created a favorable impression when guests entered the main foyer.

Thomas greeted the guests at the door. Mabelle and Dora took their coats and hats on which they pinned the names of the owners before squirreling them away in the alcove coatroom. The maids curtsied, hoping to show off their new uniforms, permed hairdos, and gleaming manicures as well as new stockings and shoes for the occasion, paid for by Miss Mona.

Mona declared even though there was a Depression, the staff didn't have to go around looking like rag-a-muffins.

Mrs. Haggin labored in the kitchen with Monsieur Bisaillon, helping Obadiah and Jedediah finish the hors d'oeuvre trays while shouting at Samuel, and Isaac to make sure the champagne flowed in the ballroom. Even Archer and other employees from the farm cheerfully helped. It was important for Miss Mona to make a good impression tonight with the bluebloods.

Dexter and Willie were the first to arrive. Willie handed her purple satin, paisley, hand-embroidered coat to Mabelle. "I'm so nervous, if anyone so much as touches me I'll jump out of my skin."

"I guess we won't be dancing then," Dexter replied sardonically.

Mabelle's hands trembled a tad when pinning Willie's name to her coat. "Know what you mean, Mrs. Deatherage, but everything should run smoothly tonight. We have extra help, and everyone has their orders."

"Hope so," Willie said. "Which way's the booze?"

Thomas replied, "We are serving champagne

on trays. An open bar has been placed in the main dining hall."

"Yummy," Willie cooed as she hurried away while Dexter stood waiting to speak with Thomas. However, he thought better of it when he saw chauffeur-driven limos pulling up.

Melanie, Miles, and Mimi came on the heels of the Deatherages. All three dumped their coats on a settee.

Dora ran over to gather them.

"Is she down yet?" Melanie asked, irritated that Mona was not present.

"I'm here, Aunt," Mona said, coming down the curved staircase. She was a shimmering vision of gold in a Charles James satin, v-neck dress covered by a filmy sheath with a leaf design in gold sequins and luminous rhinestones. A delicate mantle of the same design covering her shoulders and stopping below the bosom gave the evening gown more sparkling appeal.

"Miss Mona, you've outdone yourself!" Dexter exclaimed. He took Mona's hand assisting her down the last steps of the staircase. "Is this the young lady who used to wear rough trousers with mismatching jackets?"

"You're not wearing evening gloves," Melanie groused.

Ignoring the jibe, Mona retrieved a rare orchid corsage from a side table and graciously presented it to her aunt. "You look lovely tonight, Aunt Melanie. The men will swarm all over you like bees to a luscious flower."

Mimi fingered the gold leaf patterned sheath. "This dress must have cost a fortune."

Mona leaned over and whispered, "It did, and when you're old enough, I'll let you borrow it. Our secret, okay?"

Mimi nodded enthusiastically, so glad she had convinced her mother to allow her to attend the ball.

Melanie snapped, "People are arriving. We should be forming a reception line. Come on, Mona."

"Right behind you, Melanie."

Melanie placed herself near the front of the ballroom and pulled Mona beside her. On Mona's left stood Dexter Deatherage and a petulant Miles while Mimi was left to her own devices.

Behind the group stood Miss Jetta wearing a

new blue chiffon gown, which set off her golden brown hair. She was backup in case either Melanie or Mona forgot the names of their illustrious guests.

An eight-piece ensemble was playing Cole Porter's *Night and Day* as Melanie introduced Mona to the cream of Lexington society.

"Mona, I'd like to introduce you to the Honorable Ruby Lafoon, the Governor of the great Commonwealth of Kentucky, and his wife, Mrs. Mary Lafoon."

Mona shook their hands, "How do you do? So very nice to meet you both."

Mr. Lafoon asked, "Welcome to Kentucky, Miss Moon. How do you like our state so far?"

"The people are very friendly. I hope I can be an asset to my new home state."

"Very good to hear. I hope we may talk later."

"I would be delighted, Governor. Mrs. Lafoon."

Jetta leaned over and whispered, "Watch out for the next man in line. Mr. Chandler is a prolific hand shaker and backslapper. He's got a photographic memory and will remember everything you say and do."

Melanie shook hands with a stocky man with neatly parted black hair slicked down by pomade and winced ever so slightly by his rough, over-enthusiastic handshake. "Mona, may I present our Lieutenant Governor, Mr. Albert Chandler and his wife, Mrs. Mildred Chandler."

"Everyone calls me Happy because I'm a jolly guy," Happy Chandler announced reaching to shake Mona's hand.

Mona immediately placed her hand in front of Chandler's face to be kissed. Surprised, he grasped Mona's fingers, saying, "Enchanted," before releasing her hand.

Mona smiled sweetly. "It's a pleasure to meet you both."

Mrs. Chandler spoke up, "We knew your Uncle Manfred quite well."

"Oh."

"He was a treasured friend of ours. His passing was all so sudden, you know. We thought he was on the mend from the flu."

"Yes, Mrs. Chandler. I was quite surprised myself."

"Please call me Mildred. I hope we can become great friends."

"I do, too."

"Come on, Mildred. I see someone I want to talk to," Happy barked.

Resigned to her husband's impatience, Mildred smiled and followed her husband over to the other side of the ballroom.

Next in line was a distinguished looking gentleman with snow-white hair who shot Mona a quick appraising glance, saying, "Introduce me to your beautiful niece, Melanie." He leaned in closer causing Mona to flinch. "I see you have the characteristic Moon traits, exceptionally fair complexion, odd eye color, and platinum hair."

"Mona, may I present Dr. Henry Tuttle. He is the Moon family physician. Dr. Tuttle, this is my niece, Madeline Mona Moon."

Mona immediately recognized Dr. Tuttle's name as the signature on Uncle Manfred's death certificate. "We have almost the same color hair, Dr. Tuttle."

Chortling, Dr. Tuttle said, "It would be nice to have this color of hair if it didn't come with so many wrinkles, but you don't have to worry about that for a long time to come."

"It's so very nice to make your acquaintance.

What type of medicine do you practice?"

"I'm just an old country doctor."

Melanie cut in, "Pshaw, Henry. Why everyone in our circle depends upon you. You're a lifesaver, my knight in shining armor."

Mona resisted the urge to give Melanie a look. Was Melanie flirting with this old man, or was she just being nice? Hmm, Melanie being nice just to be nice. Nope, didn't fit.

"I hope we have a chance to chat later, Dr. Tuttle."

"I look forward to it." Dr. Tuttle quickly studied Mona's face again before moving on.

His intense scrutiny was unnerving, but Mona didn't have time to reflect on it. The receiving line was queuing up.

Jetta lightly tugged on Mona's dress and whispered, "This next man is very powerful . . . William Robertson Coe. He insured the Titanic."

Mona stepped forward. "Mr. Coe, how nice of you to come to my small soiree, especially when you have two horses running tomorrow in the Kentucky Derby—Ladysman and Pomponius."

Mr. Coe seemed astonished. "I was told you had been out of the country for a long time, and yet you know my horses?"

"I know your filly, Black Maria, won the Kentucky Oaks in 1926, the Metropolitan Handicap in 1927, and the Whitney Handicap in 1928. Your stallion Ladysman, won the 1932 Hopeful Stakes and was voted the American Champion Two-Year-Old Colt. He is the favorite to win tomorrow."

"I have two chances of winning the Derby, so I have great hopes. Please let me introduce my wife, Caroline."

"How do you do, Mrs. Coe? You know my Aunt Melanie Moon."

"I haven't had the pleasure, but William and I thank you both for the invitation. I must say you have a beautiful home, Miss Moon."

Mona ignored Melanie sniffling at that remark. "Thank you."

"Do you have a horse running tomorrow, Miss Moon?" Caroline asked.

"Call me Mona please. No such luck this year, but I am going to Churchill Downs tomorrow. Wouldn't miss the Kentucky Derby for anything. I wish you both much luck."

Mr. Coe said, "Thank you. If we don't have

another opportunity to speak tonight, we hope to
see you tomorrow."

"That would be delightful," Melanie chirped.

Caroline said, "Dear, we're holding up the
line."

"So we are. So we are."

Mona said, "Please enjoy yourselves tonight."

"We aim to," Mr. Coe said before escorting
his wife to the dance floor.

"Very well done, Miss Mona. You've impressed one of the most powerful men in the
country," Jetta assured.

"My hands are already sore from shaking, and
my dogs are barking," Mona said out of the side
of her mouth.

Melanie barked, "Shut up and smile. How do
you think I feel in these heels?"

"Steady, girls," Dexter bantered. "Here come
more fat cats. Chins up, chests out, and bottoms
tucked in."

Mona chuckled as she was introduced to more
strangers. It was another thirty-five minutes
before the line dwindled, and Melanie left to find
Mimi whom she hadn't seen since the receiving
line had formed.

Failing to locate her, Melanie implored Mona to help search, which she did. It was most fortunate that Mona found Mimi before her mother did.

19

Mona ventured on the verandah pretending to need fresh air. She was greeted by more well-wishers, but no Mimi. There were two follies on the grounds, so Mona dispatched Violet to one and she went to the other—a cottage where the family gathered for picnics in the summer. It had several chairs, a long table, and a lounging couch for those lazy afternoons where one could sneak off and read naughty books that weren't kept in one's room where the maid would find them.

Since luminaries lit the pathways, Mona had no problem making her way. Music from the ballroom floated upon the mild evening breeze as pink cherry blossoms offered up their sweet fragrance.

As Mona grew closer, she heard the faint

murmur of a man's voice imploring a giggling woman to be quiet. Mona choked down her anger as she knocked on the door and waited.

A disheveled Mimi shuffled out and stomped down three steps until she stood before Mona. "How dare you spy on me!" she hissed.

Mona smiled. A good offense was always a good defense, but Mona was not intimidated. "Let's not make a scene, dear. Hold still while I straighten your hair. Your bra strap is showing. Let me fix it. There. That looks better. Your mother is looking for you, and she's raising quite a fuss."

Mimi's eyes widened with alarm. "You won't tell?"

"Hurry, Mimi. You don't want people to know you were missing. Tongues wag, you know."

Mimi lifted her skirt and raced up the pathway toward the house. Nothing was worse than a girl's tarnished reputation in "polite society." It would ruin her chances of a suitable marriage.

Expecting a boy near Mimi's age to exit the cottage, Mona ordered, "All right young man, the coast is clear. Come out." She was prepared to give the boy a stern lecture on propriety.

The door squeaked open and out stepped a sheepish Hugh Beaumont. "It's not what it looks like."

Stunned, Mona replied hotly, "It's exactly what it looks like. Please get back inside and wait fifteen minutes while I return to the house. Go through the garden and exit the other side. I don't want my guests seeing you come up the same pathway as I."

She turned and marched up the path only to be startled by a man suddenly popping out from behind a tree. Mona instinctively reached for her gun, and when realizing she didn't possess it, decided her only recourse was to punch the man.

Staggering backwards, the man finally steadied himself and rubbed his chin. "You pack quite a wallop, Miss Mona."

"How do you know who I am?" Mona said, looking about for help.

"Because you invited me, dear lady. I was taking the air and couldn't help but witness the little debacle at the summer cottage. I ducked behind this tree so as not to embarrass little Miss Mimi scuttling back to the house. I was about to offer myself as an escort back to the ball when you attacked me."

"I attacked you? You, sir, lurched from the shadows."

"Let's start over. I'm harmless, I assure you. Let me properly present myself. I am Lord Farley."

"If you were invited, why didn't I meet you in the receiving line?"

"You can't expect an English lord to stand in a boorish queue, do you? Besides, I knew I'd meet you eventually tonight, and now I have. It's time to go back. You'll be missed, Miss Mona." Lord Farley offered his arm, which Mona reluctantly accepted.

It was at that moment Hugh Beaumont chose to leave the cottage.

Lord Farley had a look of absolute delight on his still smarting face. "Oh, this is too rich for words. The overseer shagging the granddaughter of the laird."

"Please don't say anything. I beg you, Lord Farley."

"First you pummel me. Now you're begging me."

"I'm trying so hard to make a good impression tonight, and Miss Mimi is only sixteen. Her indiscretion could ruin us both."

"Precisely. I shall have to blackmail you and extract payment."

"What!"

"For the next dance, my lady."

"Oh, is that all."

"You wound me to the quick, Madam. Is dancing with me so repugnant?"

"Must you twist my every word?"

"Don't worry. I'll keep little Miss Muffin's tryst a secret."

"Thank you. There's been enough scandal in the family."

"Are you referring to your father or your Aunt Melanie?"

"What do you mean 'Aunt Melanie?'"

"I see no one has told you the tawdry tale of Melanie's imprudent youth, but I bet she lays it on thick about your father though. I'll give you some ammunition to use against her."

"I don't like gossip."

"Oh, come now, you surely do. Everyone loves gossip as long as it isn't about themselves.

Let's just say the apple hasn't fallen far from the tree."

"I certainly don't know what you mean."

They stopped before the steps of the veran-dah. People were outside smoking and enjoying the mild evening air.

Lord Farley spoke in low tones. "When Mela-nie was a slip of a girl, she ran off with a neighbor boy. It seems the young man in question deserted Miss Melanie when he tired of her and scampered back home thinking he'd gotten off scot-free from his love adventure. That's how Daddy Dear found out his only daughter's whereabouts. Your grandfather found her in Atlantic City unmarried, pregnant, and too ashamed to come home. However, Daddy insisted upon a shotgun wedding much to the dismay of the young man and his family."

"What happened to the boy Melanie mar-ried?"

"The truth of Melanie's situation finally came out seven months later when she gave birth, and the boy's family was somewhat embarrassed. Not because their son had gotten Miss Melanie in the family way, that happens all the time, but because he had abandoned her in Atlantic City and did so again by enlisting to beat back the Germans in the Great War. Believing the Germans weren't nearly as ferocious as his young wife, he trotted bravely off to Europe, survived the war, but caught the Spanish flu in 1918 whereupon he died. So his family, not being able to stand Miss Melanie either, sold their farm and moved away. Florida, I think. Now Miss Melanie's on the prowl for husband number three."

"Three?"

"For a while she thought she could corral me, but I gave her the slip. I know all about Melanie's predatory habits. She has sharp claws."

"Who bought the boy's family farm?"

"I did, sweet lady."

"So, he was literally the boy next door. I wonder if she loved him."

"Who?"

"Melanie and her young beau. I wonder if she loved him."

"I doubt it. She was quite the lusty filly in search of a stallion." Lord Farley disparaged.

Mona winced. "That's a vulgar thing to say. You are too familiar with your opinions, sir." She moved toward the ballroom, whereupon Lord Farley grabbed her arm.

"Smile, Miss Mona. Everyone is looking at us."

Mona gave a faint grin to Lord Farley.

Lord Farley said, "You promised me a dance, and I always collect. He hustled Mona onto the ballroom floor where the musicians were playing Duke Ellington's *Sophisticated Lady* to which everyone was dancing the foxtrot. She tried to maintain distance between them, but Lord Farley pulled Mona so close, she could feel a pocket watch tick in his pocket.

Mona whispered in Lord Farley ear, "If you don't let off your vise grip, I'm going to kick you in the shin."

Lord Farley immediately loosened his hold, wondering what it would take to gain Mona's interest. "You look like a goddess in that dress all golden and shimmering."

"I think you're a swine."

"I think you're wonderful," he replied, moving about the dance floor.

"Flattery doesn't work on me, ducky."

"What does?"

"Nothing. I'm immune to your charms."

"Ah, so you think I'm charming."

When Mona didn't reply, Lord Farley asked, "Where have you been? Old Manfred never mentioned you."

"I just got back from Mesopotamia when I learned of Uncle Manfred's death."

"Trying to be another Gertrude Bell?"

"She's dead, you know, but I did work on an archeological dig which contributed several artifacts to the museum she started in Baghdad. Before that I was in London for a year, and then relocated to Berlin."

"I hear Berlin is an amusing city, especially at night."

"Berlin used to be fun, but it's getting rather dangerous due to the Nazis. The papers here don't really tell the full story of what is happening in Germany."

"Quite. My family in England is getting rather worried. They think we're going to have to fight them again sooner or later. We Brits always keep our eyes on the Huns."

Ignoring Lord Farley's chatter, Mona continued, "I returned to New York, which is my hometown, before my last assignment."

"Such a world traveler, and now you've decided to settle in little old Kentucky. We horse owners must seem dull to you after your international exploits."

"I can't tell if you're mocking me or not, so let's not talk."

"Fine with me," Lord Farley said, swirling Mona around other couples.

Mona had to admit Lord Farley was a superb dancer and soon relaxed enough to enjoy her turn about the floor. She was a bit disappointed when the song ended.

He bowed and asked, "How about riding with me to Churchill Downs tomorrow?"

"I've made arrangements to ride with the Deatherages."

"I'll meet you at your box then."

"That's impossible. I have . . ." Mona was going to say "other plans," but Lord Farley was walking away. Mona quickly turned and took a glass of champagne off a tray as Samuel passed by, hoping to appear inconspicuous.

Glancing about, she saw Dr. Tuttle sitting near several grand dames, and thought this the perfect opportunity to talk with him. She went over to the small group, asking if they needed anything.

After several minutes of small talk, Dr. Tuttle announced he was going to the verandah to smoke a cigar.

"May I join you?" Mona asked, seeing this as a perfect opportunity to speak with Dr. Tuttle privately.

"To smoke a cigar?" Dr. Tuttle asked, astounded. His old granny used to smoke a corncob pipe, and many women smoked cigarettes nowadays, but a cigar!

"It's all the rage in Paris," Mona answered, taking his arm. "Shall we?"

Once outside Dr. Tuttle said, "Thank you for getting me away from those old crows. They were complaining about everything from liver spots on their bottoms to swelling ankles. I hope you're not going to want a medical opinion. That's why I have an office. My downtime is my downtime. I need to relax." He took out a leather cigar case and silver cigar cutter from his inside pocket, pulled one out, clipped off the tip, and lit it.

Mona lowered her eyes. "I did want to speak

to you of a related medical matter that has been bothering me."

Dr. Tuttle sighed. "Let's have it."

"It concerns my uncle's death certificate. I was wondering about his broken ribs."

"Awful accident. It was the end of him. He couldn't fight those injuries and the pneumonia, too. Before the accident, Manfred was rallying. I thought he'd beat the pneumonia."

"I was wondering why he didn't ring for assistance from his bed and how he got by the nurse."

"The nurse was asleep in a chair by the bed. Perhaps he did ring for one of the servants, but they didn't respond. I've always assumed he was delirious and lost his balance, falling down the stairs."

"My butler told me the lights in the hallway had been turned off."

Dr. Tuttle shrugged. "I don't know what to tell you."

"Had Uncle Manfred been upset about anything?"

"Yes. Manfred came to see me several times before he was confined to bed. He was anxious and having trouble sleeping before he contracted the flu."

"Did he mention the source of his anxiety?"

"Manfred confided very little except he was having trouble with the family again."

"Have you any idea to whom my uncle was referring?"

"No, but I assumed it was Melanie."

"Doing what?"

"I'd rather not say."

"Did you ever suspect foul play in Manfred Moon's death?"

Dr. Tuttle drew back. "Absolutely not. I don't know what you're getting at, young woman, but it doesn't sound wholesome. Please excuse me." He threw his lighted cigar into the red azalea bushes and stormed off.

"That went well," Mona muttered, before being assailed by a group of Transylvania University professors' wives wanting Mona to join the Women's Club.

Mona nodded and said she would be delighted to attend a meeting, but was secretly hoping she would be out of town. She was dead tired, and could tell the servants were flagging as well.

Isaac whispered to her that all the food had been consumed. All of it!

There had been stuffed mushrooms, cheese wafers, pineapple-ginger shrimp, tomato aspic, breaded meatballs, pate de foie gras, deviled eggs in tomato sauce, country ham on beaten biscuits, bite-sized salmon croquettes, watercress sandwiches, fruit, petit fours, chocolate bon-bons, Ambrosia cake, and lemon tarts not to mention cases and cases of champagne, wine, and all manner of spirits.

Mrs. Haggin was so desperate she and Monsieur Bisaillon were scouring the pantry for sardines, pickles, peanut butter, crackers—anything to put on the tables.

The cream of Bluegrass society had done it. They had literally eaten Mona out of house and home. It was time for the guests to go.

If only they would!

20

"This is the Moon box," Dexter said, holding a small gate open for Mona, Willie, and Jetta to enter a private box at Churchill Downs. "Jamison, I'll take the food basket. Thank you."

"My goodness. We have seats right on the finish line," Mona said. "What luck."

Uncorking a bottle of champagne, Dexter said, "Luck has nothing to do with it. Sizable donations to Churchill Downs and the Moon name grease the wheel for the same box each year."

"I thought we're not allowed to drink liquor in public."

"No one pays any attention on Derby Day. Honey, hand me a Mint Julep and put a sprig of mint in it. It's not a Mint Julep without the mint,"

Willie said, reaching for a paper cup. "I guess that's why they call it a Mint Julep, and not just julep."

"Willie, I think you're already gassed," Mona commented, amused.

"I've been drinking steadily since last night and haven't stopped. Your party was a success. I guess you know that."

"MAY WE JOIN YOU?" a shrill voice interrupted. "After all this is the Moon box reserved for use by the Moon family."

Mona and the Deatherages looked over to see Melanie blocking the aisle, glaring at them.

"Oh God, she's got those brats with her," Willie said in a stage whisper.

"Hush, dear," Dexter admonished, taking away Willie's Mint Julep. "You've had enough to drink."

"Of course, you may join us, Melanie. All are welcomed," Mona said sweetly, making room for Melanie, Mimi, and Miles to join them.

Melanie complained, "We had to get Hugh to drive us to Louisville. It seems you absconded with Jamison and left without us."

"I'm sorry. I thought Jamison was my chauffeur."

"He's the family chauffeur," Melanie said.

"Not anymore, dear Aunt. You have more than enough money to hire your own, but as a present from me you may have any car in my garage for your own."

"What about the children?"

"What about them?"

"They both will need cars."

"I suppose you may purchase one for each of them with the money I gave you."

"They should all be our cars," Miles groused, slouching in his seat.

"Miles, I've been meaning to talk with you. Where were you the night I arrived? You were put to bed on the second floor, but when the servants went to check on you, the bed was empty."

Miles gave Mona a sly look. "What are you getting at?"

"I was wondering how you got home."

"Hello, everyone. May I join in the fun?" Hugh Beaumont asked, giving an ingratiating smile and acting as though nothing improper had happened the night before."

"I'm sorry, Hugh, but we're filled up. I see

empty seats in the grandstand though," Mona said, hoping Hugh would take the hint.

"Nonsense," Melanie said, giving Mona an irritated look. "Hugh always sits in our box. Sit here, Hugh, next to me."

There were two rows of five seats in the box with Hugh, Melanie, Miles and Dexter sitting in the lower seats while Mona, Jetta, and Willie sat above them.

"Mimi, come girl," Melanie said, beckoning.

Mimi threw a hesitant look at Mona.

"Melanie, let Mimi sit next to me. I want to ask her about the party last night."

"Yes, Mother, let me. I so want to talk about the guests with Mona."

"All right then. More room for us."

As Mona stood to let Mimi pass to an empty chair, she saw Jamison waiting against a back aisle wall. She beckoned and slipped him several dollars. "Go have fun, Jamison, but be back in three hours."

"Yes'am."

"And be sober."

Jamison said, "I never drink on the job, Miss."

"Jamison?"

"Just a little swig now and then. Keeps the cold out."

"Run along now. Remember to be back in three hours, Jamison."

Jamison tipped his hat before rushing off. "Thank you, Miss Mona."

Hugh turned around in his seat. "You shouldn't give servants money like that. It only encourages them."

"Shut up. No one asked you," Mona said. It made her furious when working people were disparaged. She had worked since she was fourteen and knew how the rich elevated themselves by denigrating the poor.

Melanie offered her opinion. "Hugh's right, Mona. They're never grateful. How much did you give Jamison? A couple of dollars, wasn't it? Too much for his kind."

Mona wanted to slap the hat off Melanie's head but refrained from doing so. She sat seething. "You do what you want with your money, and I'll do what I want with mine. Okay, Melanie?"

"Yes, but it sets a bad example for the rest of us. Servants talk, and pretty soon my help will be wanting little extras here and there."

Mona felt Jetta stiffen beside her and reached over to pat her hand. "Don't," she cautioned. "They're not worth your indignation."

Willie hiccupped, and quipped, "Melanie, why don't you wear one of those pins the Fascists are wearing in Europe now."

"Are you calling me a Red, you—you old lush?"

"Communists and Fascists are on different sides of the fence, honey. If you ever picked up a newspaper, you would know that. Tell me, do you still read with your lips moving?"

"You're ridiculous, Willie. You know that? You're turning into the town drunk. Everyone feels sorry for poor Dexter."

"Melanie, I'll be sober in the morning, but you'll still have the mind of a simpering teen in a sagging middle-aged body."

"I still have my looks."

Willie jabbed Hugh in the back of his shoulder with the toe of her shoe "Ha! Then why is your Don Juan diddling every fresh flower he comes across including last night? He took off with someone to the summer cottage. I saw them, and she looked awfully young. I just can't remember who it was? Do you, Mimi?"

Melanie jumped to her feet and swirled around, lunging at Willie or Mimi. It was hard to tell as the two were sitting next to each other. Maybe it was both.

Dexter grabbed Melanie around the waist as she struggled to slap Willie who was cackling with laughter.

Miles remained seated, paying no attention to his mother, sipping on his Coca-Cola. He was used to his mother's outbursts and was bored by them.

Mortified, Mona closed her eyes. People were gawking. She just knew it, and on the day after her triumphant entrance into Kentucky society.

"Hello. Is something amiss here?"

Mona opened her eyes to find Lord Farley with an elderly gentleman standing in the aisle next to the Moon box.

Mona stood and calmly acted as though nothing was amiss. She held her hand out to Lord Farley. "Hello. So nice to see you again." She called over her shoulder. "Melanie, look who's here. Lord Farley."

Melanie immediately stopped struggling and snarled to Dexter, "Let go of me." She patted her hair and gave a simper of a smile. "Lord Farley. Mr. Bradley. Very nice of you to stop by."

"Are we interrupting something?" Lord Farley asked, looking at a disheveled Melanie with her hat topsy-turvy.

Willie grinned at Melanie like the Cheshire Cat.

"Just the family discussing politics," Mona deadpanned.

Lord Farley gestured to the man beside him. "May I present Edward Bradley to you, Miss Moon?"

Edward Bradley leaned forward and shook Mona's hand. "I wanted to tell you how sorry I am that I missed your little gathering last night, Miss Moon, but I hear it was a success."

"Thank you, Mr. Bradley," Mona replied, remembering what Jetta had told her about his being a friend of the legendary lawman, Wyatt Earp.

"I have a horse running in the Derby, and I thought I ought to be near him last night."

"Which horse is that, sir?"

"Brokers Tip. He hasn't much of a chance. In fact, he's never won a race, but you know how it is. A horseman hates not to have a horse running in the Kentucky Derby. I don't see an entry from Mooncrest Farm."

"I think my uncle's illness precluded such business. Perhaps next year, but I wish you the best of luck today, sir."

"Luck is what I'll need with this horse. Well, I'll let you get back to your *political discussion*. I just wanted to say hello. Good day to you all," Mr. Bradley said, doffing his hat. He hurried to some friends waving to him.

Lord Farley said, "I must scoot, too. I'm sitting with Ed. Love how you're donning your hat, Melanie. Is wearing it lopsided on the side of your head the latest fashion?" He tipped his hat. "Enjoy the races, Miss Mona. Chin-chin everyone."

Mona sank back into her chair. "Oh dear, oh dear!" was all she could think to say. Why did that man always catch her family acting their worst?

However, Willie was not at a loss of words. "Meelaannieee, it seems the Big Bad Wolf and Little Red Riding Hood have flown the coop."

"What now?" Melanie screeched, sick of the Deatherages and wishing their car would drive off a cliff on the way home.

"I mean Hugh and Mimi are gone."

Mona moaned. What else could go wrong?

21

"What are you doing here? Come to gloat?" asked Mona, stepping into her drawing room.

Lord Farley feigned disappointment. "You're not very nice to me, especially when I'm doing you a favor. I'm going to a celebratory party tonight at Edward Bradley's home, and I'm allowed to bring a guest. Would you like to come?"

"Why me?"

"Why *not* you? Oh, for goodness sakes, you don't have to be suspicious all of the time, and if you show up looking as spectacular as you did at your own fete, everyone will forgive any Moon impropriety at the Derby. Besides after what happened between the jockeys of Brokers Tip and Head Play, no one will remember Melanie thrashing Wilhelmina Deatherage. The papers are calling the race "The Fighting Finish." A chap from the Courier-Journal snapped a shot of the jockeys flailing each other with their riding crops at the finish line, and it's on the front page of every newspaper in the country."

"I understand the fighting continued in the jockeys' locker room, but I can see why. I've never seen a race so close. Brokers Tip won by a nostril at most."

"If he even won. This race will be argued long after both the owners of Brokers Tip and Head Play are dead. Look, everyone will be there. You must come. Do you have another dress to wear?"

"Of course, I have," Mona snapped. "I don't know if I should leave though. Mimi has not been located yet, but keep that under your hat."

"My lips are sealed, but if I were a betting man, and I am, I should look across the border in Tennessee. That's where Kentucky couples go to elope."

"Oh, no."

"I'll pick you up at seven. It's white tie tonight, so dress to the nines. I'll see myself out."

As soon as Lord Farley left, Mona went into

the library and phoned Dexter Deatherage. "Hello, Dexter, this is Mona. Can you send some men to Jellico, Tennessee to search for Mimi? She might be in a love nest there. They must be very discreet. Very. You can? Good. Let me know if you find anything. Thank you. Good-bye."

Mona hung up wondering if Lord Farley really wanted her as his date. He was a man full of tricks. She needed to be wary of him.

Mona couldn't think about that now. She had to go over the month's budget before getting ready for Mr. Bradley's party. Mona needed to be stunning tonight. She was going to wow everyone's socks off—including the very smug Lord Farley.

22

"My dear Miss Moon. So nice to see you again."

"Mr. Bradley, congratulations on your win."

"It was a very exciting race, was it not?"

"Has your jockey recovered?"

"Minor cuts and abrasions. He'll live. Bob, glad you could come and bring the beautiful Miss Moon with you."

"Wouldn't miss this party for the world. I see you need to greet your other guests, so please excuse us as I wish to trot Mona onto the dance floor."

"Yes, everyone should see her dress. Quite daring of you, Miss Moon."

"This is the twentieth century, Mr. Bradley. Corsets have gone the way of the horse and buggy," Mona replied, referring to her bias-cut satin dress. The backless top was held in place by a strap around her neck. One side was solid white and the other black. The skirt hugged the hips and flared out at the ankles, showing off sparkly sandals. A black and white shawl around the hips provided some modesty. It was a dress meant to elicit excitement.

"A damn shame, too," Mr. Bradley said, laughing while gaping at Mona. "Go on, young people. Enjoy yourselves. Wish I was twenty years younger though. I'd give Bob a run for his money."

Lord Farley led Mona to the dance floor and twirled her about, his hand resting on her bare back.

"The great Lord Farley permits people to call him Bob?"

"Oh, shut up and dance."

"What's your full name?"

"I know your full name is Madeline Mona Moon. How come you don't have people refer to you as Madeline?"

"Because as a little girl, my playmates short-ened it to Maddy which rhymes with paddy, and the teasing never stopped. Now it's my turn. Why is an English lord mingling amongst the peasants? Did you get caught dillydallying with a duke's wife? Steal charity funds from a parish church?"

"You've caught me. I'm guilty of both."

"What's your full name?"

"Give it up. You're being a pest."

"Name, sir, or I will cause a scene."

"That seems to be a Moon specialty."

Mona stepped on his foot.

"Golly, you're such a devil. All right. If you insist, my full name is Lawrence Robert Emerton Dagobert Farley."

Mona laughed. "Dagobert. How pretentious. Do you think you are a descendant from the Merovingian kings?"

"As a matter of fact, I am a descendant of the Merovingian line, or at least, my family claims to be."

"No wonder you go by Bob Farley. I'll just call you Farley."

"At least I'm not called Dick."

"That remains to be seen."

"Now tell me why the Moons only use names beginning with the letter M," Farley asked.

"My paternal great grandmother was told by a fortune teller that wealth would remain in the family as long as all the Moon children were given names with the letter M."

"Hogwash."

"I agree, but why tempt fate?"

"So tell me, Madeline Mona Moon, what does a lady cartographer do?"

"Same as a male cartographer. I've mapped out areas for exploring expeditions and archeological adventures—that type of thing. I've even worked on proposed dams and roads."

"So you're basically a surveyor."

"It's a little more involved than that. I make maps and charts for others to use."

"Miss the excitement?"

"I miss the exploring, but it was hard, boring work with bad food, beastly weather, and uncooperative male assistants."

"With your money, you can underwrite your own expeditions to anywhere in the world. You might even find King Solomon's mines."

"You're making fun of me again, but wherever there is a legend, there is a grain of truth. Look at Heinrich Schliemann finding Troy and the treasure of Priam, or Howard Carter discovering the tomb of Tutankhamun."

Lord Farley decided to change the subject. "There's a blue moon tonight. Did you notice?"

"A second full moon in a thirty day period."

"Magic happens on the second full moon. People fall in love."

"Really? I don't see what a full moon has to do with anything."

"Can't you play along?"

"I haven't the talent for romance. I'm too practical."

"Just follow my direction."

"Well, you're leading."

"Have I told you that you smell divine?"

"It's a new perfume called Vol de Nuit."

"Night Flying. A strange name for a perfume. Next time put some droplets in your hair."

"Whatever for?"

"Because of this." Farley pulled Mona against him, pressing his cheek against hers as they spun around the room.

Mona didn't resist Farley's familiarity this time, feeling a sudden jumble in her stomach. She was surprised at how readily she yielded. It lasted only a few seconds but felt like being on a roller coaster. Being close to Farley felt good, even though she knew he must be a bounder. She had a friend, Lady Alice, in England whom she would write to about this Lawrence Robert Emerton Dagobert Farley. If Bob Farley had a past, her friend would know it.

Until Mona received a letter from her friend, Lady Alice, telling her what's what with Farley, she decided to have fun with him—something Mona had very little of in her life.

23

Mona went to the dining area for a glass of punch while Farley and a group of men surrounded Don Meade, Brokers Tip's jockey, as he recounted *the fighting finish* for the umpteenth time.

Bored with the constant retelling of the race, Mona wandered off in search of refreshment, bumping into Happy Chandler's wife.

"Mildred, how nice to see you again."

"Mona, my goodness, what a dress you're wearing."

"Yes, I understand it's a little risqué for Kentucky."

"If I had your figure, I'd wear it. You're only young once."

Mona protested, "But you're young."

"Once a woman has children, such clothes are a thing of the past. I see you came with Lord Farley. He's a good-looking man in a smart package—all that dark hair. Reminds me of Clark Gable."

"You think? I thought he looked like a pirate." Mona dabbed some shrimp salad on a plate. "Know about him—anything I should watch out for?"

"Only that he has impeccable manners, good teeth, lots of money, and claims he's the son of a duke or something."

"Why's he over here then? Shouldn't he be in England lording his status over his inferiors?"

"That's what I've asked my husband, but since Farley contributes to my husband's campaigns, I'm told not to look a gift horse in the mouth."

"Your husband is ambitious."

"Very, but he's a good man and really wants to help folks. He means to run for governor, and if he wins, he'll make a good one."

"Why stop at governor?"

Mildred laughed. "That's what he says."

"You told me you were close to my uncle. I understand there was a falling out between Aunt

Melanie and Uncle Manfred. Can you tell me anything about it?"

Mildred pulled Mona aside and out of earshot. "I'm very fond of Melanie. I know you must think her a silly woman, but Melanie has had to withstand blows most of us never face. She's been badly used and has never had time to recover before the next storm heads her way. God bless her."

"For instance?" Mona asked.

"I'd rather not say, but much of it involved trusting the wrong person. Of course, we all saw her take a swing at Wilhelmina Deatherage at the Derby. This type of behavior certainly does her no credit. I imagine it's why she's not here tonight. Her conduct would have been the talk of the town if those two jockeys' beating each other with their riding crops hadn't been worse."

"But why did Melanie and Manfred fall out?"

"I don't know if it is my place to say."

"Please, Mildred. I need help if I'm to make a go of it here. No one will tell me anything, and quite frankly, I'm stumbling in the dark."

Mildred gave a sympathetic look. "I'll tell you the rumor, but I don't believe a word of it.

Manfred believed Melanie was embezzling money by forging his name on checks."

"Was that a year ago?"

"Yes. They had a huge falling out about it, and Manfred banned Melanie and the children from Moon Manor."

"Was there money missing?"

"According to him—yes. Even if there were missing funds, I doubt it was Melanie's doing."

"Why is that?"

"Because she is not a thief. It isn't her nature, besides she has plenty of money."

"Not to hear Melanie tell it," Mona said.

"Oh, I know Melanie is always crying poor mouth, but she has plenty. When her husband died, she received quite a bequeathal, so she has no need of money. Men are her weakness, but Melanie has never stolen another woman's beau or had an affair with a married man. If embezzlement did take place, I would take a hard look at her son, Miles. It was no secret he wanted to be master of Mooncrest Farm and was vocal that he needed a larger allowance. Perhaps he decided to help himself."

"I can tell he's bitter that I inherited the estate."

"You did come out of nowhere, my dear. All I can say is be careful of him. It was a shock when he learned he was never to inherit Mooncrest Farm, and the surprise has turned into a festering wound."

"What are you ladies whispering about?" Farley asked, appearing flushed and sporting a crooked tie.

Mildred answered, "Just girl talk. Please excuse me. I need to find my husband."

"Was it something I said?" Farley asked Mona.

"Calm down. The world doesn't revolve around you."

"It doesn't?"

"Take me home before you become so smashed, you can't see the road. Better yet, I'll drive."

Farley protested, "It's still the shank of the evening."

"It's over for you, *Lord Bob*. Let's go. I'll say our goodbyes to Mr. Bradley while you order the car."

"Woman, you are a bossy wench."

"I know. It's one of my most redeeming qualities."

"Who told you that lie?"

"Shall I call for a cab?"

"No. No. I'll take you home, but we're going to miss the best part of the party."

Unrelenting, Mona went in search of Edward Bradley. She wanted to get home and go through the bank statement along with the letters she had found on the day of her arrival.

Mona had always wondered why Uncle Manfred had kept such items in his bedroom.

Now she believed those items held the key to her uncle's death.

24

Mona inspected the great mahogany desk in the library with her magnifying glass and found minute scratches near the drawer locks. "This is why Uncle Manfred didn't trust his desk and kept important documents in his room. Someone pried the drawers of his desk open," she muttered, ringing for Jetta.

"Yes, Miss Mona. You called for me?"

"Where did Uncle Manfred keep his checkbook, Jetta?"

"In the desk drawer."

"Always?"

"Yes."

"Did he keep it locked?"

"Yes, he kept the key on his watch fob."

"He didn't have a safe?"

"I was never aware of one."

"I can't seem to find his checkbook. Do you know where it is?"

"Mr. Deatherage has it."

"Another thing. I can't find any of Uncle Manfred's correspondence after 1931."

"Mr. Deatherage had the post office forward all of the estate's mail to his office."

"Why?"

"You need to ask him, Miss."

"I'm asking you."

Jetta shifted her feet uncomfortably. "Mr. Moon and Mr. Deatherage believed it was in the best interest of the estate if the checkbook was locked in Mr. Deatherage's office, and his staff review all of Mr. Moon's mail."

"Why was that?"

"I hesitate to say."

"It wouldn't be because Uncle Manfred believed his sister, Melanie, was embezzling from the estate, and he felt someone was going through his private papers?"

Jetta grew wide-eyed. "How did you hear?"

Mona took this as confirmation of what Mildred Chandler had told her. "So it's true. Is that why Melanie and her children were asked to leave Moon Manor?"

"Yes, but Mr. Deatherage couldn't prove Miss Melanie was the culprit."

"Who else was suspected?"

"All of the servants were questioned, even myself I'm ashamed to say."

"Since no one has been fired, I take it nobody took the blame—or has someone been let go?"

"No one, Miss Mona. I assure you."

"Jetta, besides Mr. Deatherage, no one knew Uncle Manfred's business like you did. Was someone blackmailing him?"

"He became anxious and was secretive, but I was not privy to Mr. Moon's thoughts, let alone his secrets."

"Let me assure you that I don't appreciate information kept from me. I've been met with nothing but resistance from the staff regarding my uncle's demise, and I'm tired of it. If you wish to continue here, you'd better speak up. I don't like to be kept in the dark."

"I understand. Is that all?"

Mona sighed. "You may go." She hated being harsh with Jetta, as she thought her secretary to be a kind, thoughtful person, but something was not right at Moon Manor, and Mona was determined to ferret it out.

25

Violet had gone to her mother's for the afternoon, so Mona had Dora bring up a tray and stated she wasn't feeling well and would not be down for dinner. This gave Mona time to study Uncle Manfred's records without being disturbed.

Rain beating against the window competed with the sound of a warm fire crackling in the fireplace. Chloe snuggled asleep against Mona who nibbled on finger sandwiches and teacakes while perusing her uncle's belongings.

The bank statement was dated December 1931 and showed a series of withdrawals numbering three hundred, seven hundred, and a whopping one thousand three hundred dollars circled in red ink. Mona assumed that is when Uncle Manfred noticed something was awry.

The letters were dated from 1932 to a week before Manfred's death. They were mostly from Dexter replying to Uncle Manfred's questioning the withdrawals from his personal account and those from Moon accounts.

Apparently Dexter had closed all Moon checking accounts and opened new ones with both his and Uncle Manfred's signatures required on the checks. There was a letter from Dexter stating he could not read Uncle Manfred's handwriting. Did her uncle avoid using Miss Jetta to type the letters because he didn't trust her?

Hmm.

Another letter discussed auditing Melanie's expenses, but there was a curious note about Archer. It said that Dexter had investigated Archer's earlier employment with other divisions in Moon Enterprises and that Manfred should be shed of him. Dexter was to speak of this investigation when next they met, but Uncle Manfred died before then.

Mona put the letters aside and took up the calendar. There were several dates with red circles and notes beside the days such as *food poisoning, car brakes failed*, or *don't want to be alone.*

It was obvious Dexter knew much more than he was telling her making Mona furious. She would talk to Dexter tomorrow afternoon after her riding date with Farley in the morning.

A date she was not going to miss!

26

"How do I look?" Mona asked Farley.

"Smashing, but perhaps a little overboard."

Mona looked down at her riding outfit. "Whatever is wrong with it? It was all the rage in England last year."

"That's the problem. You look like you're going on an English fox hunt. The only thing missing is a veil and the side saddle."

Mona felt deflated. "I'm never going to fit in."

"Yes, you will. Let's take off the jacket. It's warm, and we're just going for a pleasure ride. You don't need it."

Mona let Farley help remove her wool jacket. "When did you arrive?"

"Shortly before you did. The horses were already saddled."

"I hope the grooms have picked out a gentle one for me. I'm hardly an accomplished equestrienne."

"I'm sure they did as you told them. The gelding seems spirited, so I'll ride him. You take the mare. I hope you don't mind me suggesting this outing."

"Not at all. I need the exercise, but I need to be in town this afternoon. I have an appointment."

"Then let's get you on." Farley held the horse's bridle while Mona let the stable boy help her up the mounting steps. A beautiful roan mare with soft brown eyes waited patiently.

No sooner had Mona settled in the saddle than the horse snorted and bucked, launching Mona into the air. The horse reared, allowing Farley a few short seconds to pull the astonished stable boy out of the way of the horse's hooves. Mona was not so lucky. The horse turned her fury on Mona lying stunned and helpless on the ground. Coming to her senses, Mona barely dodged the mare's sharp hooves.

Excited by the commotion, the gelding kicked as well. Farley untied its reins and slapped the horse on the rump, allowing it to gallop off. He hoped the angry mare would follow.

She did.

Rushing over, Farley blurted out, "Mona! Mona! Are you all right? Speak to me, darling."

Mona opened her eyes. "Why are you weaving, Farley? Stop that."

Farley ordered the groom. "Get Jamison. Miss Mona's going to the hospital. Then capture that horse and see what the matter is."

"Must be she ate jimson weed, sir."

Farley didn't answer as he picked Mona up and hurried toward Moon Manor.

27

Dr. Tuttle looked at the hospital chart. "You've suffered a nasty fall, but I'm sending you home. Someone should be with you at all times for the next twenty-four hours."

"Why is my left side so sore?"

"From the bruise pattern, it looks like a glancing blow from the horse's hoof. Mooncrest Farm seems to be having problems with its horses. First Boller. Now you. Take it easy for the next week or so. Plenty of rest. That sort of thing. I'll check on you at Moon Manor in a couple of days."

Mona struggled to sit up. "How am I to get home?"

"I've seen to it," Lord Farley said, stepping out from the shadows in a corner. "Jamison is here with the car and the nurse and I will help you into a wheelchair."

Mona lay back down. "Do you mind if we wait? I'm suddenly dizzy."

Dr. Tuttle tapped the side of his leg impatiently. "Well, I'll be off then. I see you have plenty of help."

"Thank you, Dr. Tuttle."

"Yes, thank you," Lord Farley murmured.

A nurse brought in a wheelchair.

"Can you give us a minute, please?" Lord Farley requested.

Without saying a word, the nurse stepped out from the room.

"Mona, try sitting up. I'll help you."

"I seem to remember you calling me darling?"

"Don't be a goose. Absolutely not."

"You did. I heard you."

"Head trauma, Mona. Cuckoo. Come on now. Sit up, girlie."

"You like me."

"Don't be a silly cow. I loathe you."

"Ah, you called me a cow. That's the British equivalent of 'I love you.'"

"Mona, please let me help into the wheelchair,

so Jamison and I can get you home."

"What happened? I remember some of it."

"No sooner had you rested your bum in the saddle, the mare threw you off like a rag doll. It was most extraordinary to see you fly through the air."

Farley leaned over Mona and put his arms around her with the expectation of lifting her off the bed, but Mona put her face close to his. "Kiss me."

"What!"

"I know you want to kiss me. Do it."

"I certainly do not want to kiss you, you brazen harlot."

"Is there a Mrs. Lord Farley?"

"Noooo."

"Then what's the problem?"

"You're woozy and you stink."

"I beg your pardon," Mona protested.

"You smell of horse manure."

"I must have rolled in some. I bet I look a fright."

"Not too bad, considering." Farley brushed Mona's lips with his.

She closed her eyes thinking he was really

going to kiss her when she heard him say, "Nope, sorry. You really do reek."

"Oh, you're horrid."

"Upsy-daisy, now. That's a good lass. Into the wheelchair. Jamison will get you home in no time, and you take a long soak in the tub and then scoot off to bed."

Mona grabbed Farley's hand. "Bob, don't let my men shoot that mare. Find out what happened."

"I intend to, my repellent little flower. I almost got my head bashed in, too."

Mona didn't respond, as she had fallen asleep.

Farley didn't have the heart to shake her, but she had to stay awake for the next several hours.

He called the nurse for the distinct pleasure of letting her incur Mona's wrath. Watching the nurse stoically bear Mona's epitaphs after shaking her awake, Farley wondered what was rotten in Moon Manor.

First it was Manfred who was involved in several accidents and then his death. Then Mr. Boller was hurt in a freak accident. Now Mona. His maid, via gossip from Moon Manor's Dora, related someone had tried to break into Mona's room in the middle of the night, and Mona had fended him off with a gun. *Attagirl, girl, Mona.*

Still, something wasn't right, and that something almost got his head staved in. Farley liked keeping his head intact, thank you very much.

What was required was a little snooping of his own.

28

"Good morning," Lord Farley said, striding into Mona's bedroom several days later.

Violet almost dropped a coffee pot. "You shouldn't be in Miss Mona's boudoir, Lord Farley. What would people say?"

"I don't know. What would people say, Violet?"

Buttering some toast, Mona spoke up, "What difference does it make? Visitors have been tramping into my room lately. I can hardly get any rest."

"I was told your bedroom door was always locked."

"Who told you? Oh, never mind. There's no privacy in this house or in this town as far as I can tell. If you must know, it was just too hard on

Violet to keep locking and unlocking the door, so we left it open—thus all the visitors barging in for a quick howdy-do."

"Who's been here?" Farley asked pulling a chair up to the bed.

"The Deatherages. Melanie. Jetta. Mildred Chandler. Mrs. Boller. Ladies from the Lexington Women's Club. Even Mr. Bradley. That reminds me—where have you been the last several days?"

"Sleuthing on your behalf."

"Tell me first. My horse, does it yet live? I hate to have it put down on my account. I must have jabbed it in a soft spot with my boots."

"It had nothing to do with you."

"Then what was it?"

Farley paused, glancing at Violet.

Mona knew he wanted to talk with her privately. "Violet, be a dear and fetch me some scones. I can smell them all the way from the kitchen."

"They are for tea time, Miss."

"I would like some now."

"Monsieur Bisaillon won't like it."

"He'll get over it, and bring Lord Farley a cup and saucer. I'm sure he wants some scones and coffee, too."

After Violet scurried to the kitchen, Farley strode over to the door and looked in the hallway. He wanted to make sure no one overheard their conversation. Scooting the chair closer to the bed, he picked up a piece of toast and took a bite. "This would taste better with marmalade."

"Oh, get on with it," Mona complained.

"I went to talk with the stable boy. He said the two horses were already saddled when he arrived at work. He assumed I had come earlier and saddled them myself."

Mona smacked Farley's hand when he tried to snatch more toast. "Leave my toast alone."

"You're getting fussy over a bit of bread?"

"What about my horse?"

"Your men located her on the road. She had jumped a fence and was a wild thing. They finally got her calmed down and brought back to the stable where they found this stuck to the underside of the saddle blanket." He dropped what appeared to be a spiked, oval-shaped seedpod into Mona's hand.

"How devilishly clever—a cocklebur!"

"Some fiend took a knife and scraped a raw

spot on the horse's back and placed the cockle-bur under the saddle blanket where the wound was. Imagine the pain when a rider put his weight on it. Any horse would go berserk."

"No wonder she tried to throw me off. Poor thing. Tell me a vet has seen her."

"She's on the mend, but quit worrying about the horse and worry about yourself. I think the incident involving your man Boller was a trial run."

"Boller wasn't riding the horse. He's a groom."

"He was washing the horse when it went crazy."

"Was it the same horse?"

"No, but it had a similar abrasion on it."

"How would this someone know which horse I was to ride that morning?"

"Someone sneaked in to saddle those particular horses. It makes sense you would take the smaller mare, and I would take the larger gelding. I'm the more experienced horseman. What have you ever ridden with ease? Camels?"

"How would they even know I was riding that morning?"

"Haven't you been complaining that everyone knows your business?"

"True. I suppose one of the servants heard me talking with you on the telephone. It would only take minutes to go through the servant grapevine."

"Who resents you?"

"Umm, let's see. The entire staff especially Mrs. Haggin. Melanie. Miles. Probably Archer. He can't look at me without scowling."

"It has to be someone familiar with the estate and horses."

"That's everyone, Farley."

"Yes."

"Let me ask you something. Do you find anything odd about my uncle's death?"

"I saw him the day before the accident. He was rallying—getting better. Then he plummeted down the stairs and that was that."

"I don't think the fall was accidental, but by design."

"How do you mean?"

"Not sure, but I'm working on a theory."

"This is bad business. The Moon money is not worth your life," Farley warned.

"Someone thinks it is. My father was forced to give up his inheritance, but I refuse to cower."

"Mona, trust no one."

"Not even you?"

"Especially not me." Farley stood up abruptly, passing Violet on the way out.

"Is Lord Farley coming back?" asked Violet, holding a tray of scones and an extra teacup.

Mona looked thoughtful. "I don't know, Violet, but I hope so. For the first time in my life, I do hope so."

29

Bored silly from mandatory bed rest, Mona had Violet bind her ribs in gauze and help her dress. The day before, Mona had instructed Jetta to track down the night nurse's address. She was determined to speak with her.

"Should you be going off on your own?" Violet said, helping Mona gather her purse and gloves.

"Jamison will drive me." Mona stopped and had a thought. "Would you like to come, Violet? Be Watson to my Sherlock Holmes."

"Oh, yes." Violet's blue eyes brightened at the prospect of an adventure.

"Change out of your uniform, but hurry. I'll meet you down at the car."

Violet jumped at the chance and rushed to her

room, throwing off her uniform on the way.

Mona smiled seeing Violet so excited. Still not steady on her feet, she grabbed one of the many canes accumulated over the years at Moon Manor and got into the elevator, doubting she would ever take the stairs again until she learned who had harmed her uncle and brought on his demise.

By the time Mona reached the front door, Violet rushed down the staircase while hurriedly putting on hcr hat and gloves. "Let me help you," Violet insisted, getting on one side of Mona.

Jamison rushed up the portico steps to assist Mona as well.

"This is so silly," Mona said, embarrassed. "But thank you. I have a fear of falling."

"Better safe than sorry, Miss Mona," Jamison insisted, helping her ease into the back seat of the Daimler.

Violet got in beside Mona and laid a blanket over her lap.

Mona didn't like being treated like an invalid but said nothing. If Violet liked to fuss, let her. The only people in Mona's life who had given her any nurturing attention had been her parents. Mona had to admit she was still terribly bruised and not as confident as before the accident. However, the little revolver in her purse made Mona feel somewhat in charge.

Violet handed Jamison the address and was humming with enthusiasm.

"Violet, I have something to ask you. Please don't take offense, but I've noticed you sometimes use the wrong verb tense in your sentences, but utter words like 'mar.'"

Violet turned a bright crimson red. "I'm sorry if I shame you, Miss. I know servants are not to speak in the same manner as their betters."

"*Their betters*? Oh, dear. I see Lord Farley has corrupted the countryside with his English snobbery."

"When I hear someone say a word I don't know, I look it up in the library's great dictionary, and then I try to use it."

"Bravo for you, Violet. I'm a great believer in women's education."

Violet turned away and stared out the window.

"Violet, have I upset you?"

"You'd better know. I never graduated from high school. I wanted to finish, but my family needed money, so I had to work."

"Did Uncle Manfred know you left school?"

"He never asked."

"Hmm. I'm beginning to see the lot of common folk here alarmingly similar to those in other countries, but things are quickly advancing for the working woman."

"Do you mean unions, Miss? Don't even say the word. You'll get your head busted, or worse you'll be shunned by the swells."

"Things are changing in this country, Violet. People are demanding their rights to good pay, adequate housing, and education for their children. The Great War put an end to the era of the robber baron."

"You sound like one of them radicals."

"I suppose I do. We'll discuss the labor movement again after you've finished high school. I'll speak with Miss Jetta. She'll know how to proceed with your education."

"How can I study with my work hours? I need this job, Miss Mona. Please don't take it from me."

Alarmed at Violet's plea, Mona assured, "Violet, don't worry. We working gals must stick together. I understand the need for employment. Really I do. Trust me on this matter."

The car stopped in front of a modest white framed house with blue shutters.

"Ah, we're here. Stay in the car, Violet. This shouldn't take too long."

Jamison opened Mona's door and helped her out.

"Thank you, Jamison. I'll be fine." Mona went to the front door and knocked on the door with the brass end of the cane. Hearing a rustling inside, Mona waited patiently until a small bird of a woman with coal black hair opened the door.

"Good morning. I'm Mona Moon. Would this be the home of Aurora Prather?"

"It might be," Mrs. Prather replied, peeking at Jamison and the Daimler. "You must be the new mistress at Moon Manor. Heard about you. What a lucky gal you are!"

"May I come inside, Mrs. Prather? I wish to talk to you about my uncle's death."

The nurse eyed Mona suspiciously "Come to chastise me?"

"I'm after information. Please let me come in and sit. I feel almost faint."

Alarmed at Mona's wan complexion, Mrs. Prather grew concerned. She was a nurse after all, and her training kicked in. She helped Mona to a rocking chair before a small fire. "Let me make some coffee. You look done in."

"No thank you. I shall be here only a short while."

Mrs. Prather stood before Mona, clasping her hands. "Well, what do you want?"

"Can you go over the night my uncle fell down the stairs?"

"There ain't much to say. It was horrible, let me tell you. Him screaming in pain, although I think it was more shock than anything."

"Were you surprised when Mr. Moon died?"

"Yes. Everyone talks about how old Mr. Moon was when he passed, but he wasn't feeble at all. He was in his fifties, for goodness sake. Even with his injuries, Mr. Moon should have recovered."

"Did the doctor order an autopsy?"

"I wouldn't know. I had been let go by then."

"Because you fell asleep."

"Drugged was more like it. Somebody slipped me a Mickey Finn. I complained to the doctor, but he wouldn't listen. He said I was making up a story to save my job. I never had a mishap before. I always put my patients first."

"Who was at the house that night?"

"The regular staff who lived at Moon Manor. Mr. Moon had several visitors that evening. Let me see—I seem to recall Mr. Deatherage visiting. Then Miss Melanie with her son, Miles. I thought their visit peculiar because young Miles stood out in the hallway speaking with Archer. He never came in to see his uncle."

"Were Archer and Miles always friendly?"

"I never knew them to be."

"Your routine was regular except for the visitors?"

"I got Mr. Moon settled, and that's all I remember until Samuel woke me up. I had a terrible headache."

"What is the very last thing you remember, Mrs. Prather?"

"I was drinking tea."

"Where was the cup after you were awakened?"

"It had fallen to the floor."

"Too bad we don't have it."

"But I do, Miss Moon. Please don't think I stole it to be stealing, but after Dr. Tuttle thought I had sloughed off my duties, I took the cup, thinking it might prove my innocence someday."

"May I have it? I would like to have it tested."

"Would you? I would give anything to have my good name restored."

"I can't promise anything, but I'll see what I can do."

"Wait here," Mrs. Prather said, rushing off to collect the cup.

Mona pulled out a little diary from her purse and scribbled notes. The pieces of the puzzle were starting to fall into place.

30

Mona returned to the car with a small bag in her hand with the teacup securely wrapped. Her talk with Mrs. Prather only heightened her suspicions and she decided to press Jamison for information on the drive home.

"Jamison, how many cars are there in the garage?"

"Five, Miss. The farm has ten vehicles, mostly trucks for various purposes."

"Are you responsible for the farm trucks?"

"Mr. Beaumont has his own man for them."

"Has there been any trouble with the vehicles in the past year?"

"How do you mean?"

"Accidents with Mr. Moon in the car?"

"We had one. The brakes went out, but I got

the car to roll to a stop." Jamison laughed. "A maple tree helped. Did a little damage to the chrome but not much."

"Why did the brakes go out?"

"No brake fluid. I checked everything else. The line was good, but no fluid. I've never understood it either, because I check the oil, transmission and brake fluids every month. I couldn't figure it out."

"Did you always drive Uncle Manfred?"

"He liked to drive himself sometimes if the weather was good."

"Did he drive the Daimler?"

"No Miss. He would take the Pontiac Roadster. He liked to drive with the top down."

"Did you check the brake fluid in the Phaeton?"

"Yes, Miss. There was a little hole in the brake line. It was the darndest thing."

"Did you report back to my uncle?"

"He got skittish. I could tell he was fretting about it."

"What did he say?"

"Nothing. Didn't say a word to me."

"Did you keep driving him after the accident?"

"Yes, but I checked the oil and brake fluid every day thereafter."

"Did he ever drive by himself again?"

"No. He said it gave him no pleasure to drive anymore."

"Don't you think it was odd the brakes didn't work on two cars in which Mr. Moon was a regular passenger?"

"Not my place to say."

"But you have thoughts about it, surely?"

"Not my place to say," Jamison repeated.

Violet asked, "Why not?"

"Because it's white folks business. Best for a man like me to keep his thoughts to himself."

Mona understood Jamison's reluctance. She had read in a history of Lexington there had been an attempted lynching of a black man by a drunken mob as recently as thirteen years ago. Apparently, the Civil War had done nothing to dismiss Kentucky's social prejudices and Jim Crow laws made matters worse. Mona had been to many countries where people were oppressed by an unyielding ruling class, so she did not press the matter.

Believing Jamison was finished speaking, she

let him help her out of the Daimler when he whispered, "Old Scratch has done his devil work with the Moon family ever since your father was cast out, and he's fight'n to stay put. Beware, Miss Mona. Beware!"

31

Dexter leapt from his desk to greet Mona. "What a pleasant surprise. I thought you'd still be recuperating." He pulled up a chair for Mona and sat on the edge of his desk.

"I have a burr under my saddle, no pun intended, and I'm not happy. In fact, I think I have been lied to and kept in the dark about important matters at Moon Manor. If you thought you could keep me compliant as you do Willie by plying her with liquor, you are sadly mistaken."

Dexter paused momentarily, taken aback. "That's a very unkind thing to say about Wilhelmina."

Mona took off her gloves, folding them into her clutch. "Yes, but there it is. You must think me stupid."

"I think of neither you nor my wife as stupid. Willie is struggling at the moment, and you are never to speak of her in that manner again. I love my wife and when push comes to shove, I'll drop you like a hot potato if you ever insult her good name again."

Mona smiled. "I was hoping you would defend Willie and threaten to give me the boot."

"I admit I have kept things from you, but I did it to protect the Moon family. If you didn't have any preconceived notions, then settling in would be easier."

"No more, Dexter. You must be direct and truthful. Something is not right at Moon Manor, and I feel my life could be in danger."

"What do you want me to do?"

"Tell me why Uncle Manfred selected me as his heir. It wasn't due to his tender feelings toward me."

Dexter paused. He wasn't sure how to put into words Manfred Moon's concerns. "Manfred believed Melanie was embezzling from his personal account. Miles had been on the warpath for an increase in his allowance, and Manfred nixed the idea."

"Melanie has her own money from her husband's estate, so why would Miles have to crawl to Manfred?"

"It seems Melanie's second husband gambled much of Melanie's fortune away before he dropped dead of dropsy."

"Two dead husbands. Should I say I'm sorry?"

"Heaven's no. Everyone despised him, including Melanie."

"Was there proof of Melanie's deceit?"

"It was all conjecture. Melanie knew where Manfred kept the checkbook, and the handwriting on the checks was similar to Melanie's. The month before the checks were written, she had a quarrel with Manfred over money. He accused Melanie of being a spendthrift, and she called him a penny-pinching, money-grubbing brother. You see where it led."

"To Manfred being predisposed to believe his baby sister was helping herself to the cookie jar."

"Correct. After it was confirmed the checks had been forged, Manfred ordered Melanie and the children to move and banned them from Moon Manor. To the outside world, the Moon family seemed happy and contented, but to those who knew, the family was bitterly divided."

"Anyone could have forged Uncle Manfred's name. Jetta for one."

"We considered her. She had an account at Manfred's bank and, as he was a trustee, it was easy enough to look at her account. No sizeable deposits."

"Did you search her room?"

"Nothing out of the ordinary, except we discovered she was reading *Lady Chatterley's Lover.*"

When Mona did not react to Jetta's preference of reading material, Dexter hurried on. "I did not think Jetta was a likely suspect."

"What about Miles?"

"If that boy had an idea, it would die of loneliness. I never considered him."

"Any description of who cashed the checks?"

"The checks were taken to a sister bank in Covington. The tellers can't remember who cashed them."

"Surely with such large amounts, the bank investigated the account? Wasn't there suspicion when the checks were not deposited?"

"The checks were made out to various firms

with which we do business, and the amounts were not unusual. No alert had been issued, and the bank does a high volume business. They think nothing of handing over large amounts of money since lots of businesses pay their employees in cash."

"So who then?"

"I don't know. When Manfred threatened to disinherit Melanie, I knew he meant it, so I went in search of you as the next in line. Manfred only had your mother's old address, but we caught the New York Times article stating you were a guest of Lady Alice Morrell in Great Britain last year. We tracked you from there, and I had detectives investigate you. Their report said you were even tempered, educated, unattached, and hard working—a perfect candidate to watch over the Moon fortune. I thought you a godsend."

"Uncle Manfred didn't really want me to be heir, because he waited until the last moment to change his will."

Dexter said, "He did."

"But I was his last choice."

"What difference does it matter how you became heir? You are, and you should run with it."

"You forget someone is trying to kill me."

"I think that mausoleum you live in has you spooked. Nobody is trying to kill you. You have a case of the nerves."

Pursing her lips, Mona studied Dexter. She liked him and he was good at his job, but Dexter lacked imagination. It was beyond the pale that anyone would want to murder in Dexter's comfortable middle class world, so therefore murder was something that happened to others—strangers, not people he knew. "I found one of your letters to Manfred warning him to fire Archer. Why?"

"Archer worked for your uncle in another capacity before he came to Moon Manor. All I wish to say on the matter is he was extremely effective in persuading union organizers to leave our miners be. I found his history to be one of violence and drink. I didn't think him suitable to work at Moon Manor. I don't even know how he got the job."

"He was a head buster."

"That's one way of putting it."

"Is there anything else to add to this tawdry story?"

Glancing at his watch, Dexter said, "I'm sure there is, but darned if I can think of it now."

"It had to be someone who knew the inner workings the estate—Jetta, Miles, Mrs. Haggin, or Melanie. What about Hugh Beaumont?"

"Thought of him, but couldn't find anything."

"That leaves you, Dexter."

"You're not serious?"

Mona rose to leave. "Thank you for allowing me to take up your time."

"I feel the swipe of a claw."

"Now who's paranoid?" Mona asked.

Dexter followed Mona out into the reception room where Violet was waiting. The three of them made their way to the Daimler, where Dexter helped Mona into the car.

She could tell Dexter was glad to see the back of her but didn't care because Chloe and a long nap awaited her. Mona would lock herself in tonight, but she couldn't stay locked up forever. Sooner or later, Mona was going to have to face the music and point her conductor's baton at the culprit.

It would be a nasty business.

32

Later that week Mona strode past two Pinkerton detectives into the library.

Mimi jumped to her feet. "You have no right to drag us back here. We're married. See!" She pulled a certificate from her purse.

Taking the marriage license, Mona studied it. Handing it back, she said, "It looks legal, but that's not the issue."

Wrapping his arm around Mimi, Hugh said, "We're man and wife now, and there's nothing you can do about it."

"Mimi is sixteen. She did not have her mother's permission to marry. Melanie can have the marriage annulled."

"That will be a bit awkward as the marriage has been consummated," Hugh replied, elbowing a giggling Mimi.

"I see. What about school, Mimi?"

"Who cares? I'm married now." She gave her husband a quick peck on the cheek.

"It doesn't bother you that Hugh was wooing your mother before he took up with you?"

"Where is Mother? Why isn't she here?"

Ignoring Mimi, Mona said, "Melanie has been deeply hurt by you, Mr. Beaumont. She thought you were on the level."

"Melanie will get over it. In fact, we going to head over to see her once this meeting is over."

"Yes, you can't hold us here. It's kidnapping," Mimi complained. "Those awful men in the hallway just barged into our room. Next thing we knew, we were hustled into a car and brought here."

"I don't think there's a judge in the county who might agree that a thirty-two-year-old man has the right to steal away a sixteen-year-old girl."

Hugh protested, "Mimi came of her own free will. She was not coerced. Many girls get married at her age."

"That's right," Mimi agreed. "I love Hugh."

"But does he love you?"

"Of course, I do," Hugh said, smiling at his young bride.

Mimi giggled, and it was all Mona could do to not roll her eyes.

"That may be, but let's talk about some practical matters. How are you going to support Mimi, Hugh?"

"I haven't thought about it. I wonder if you would be a doll and let me have my old job back?"

Mona remained silent.

"We'll go to Mother's and stay with her. Hugh won't have to work. He's a Moon now. The Moon money will take care of us."

"I control the Moon money, and it will not go to support the two of you."

Mimi snarled, "Mother has money of her own. We don't need you."

"Ah, there's the rub, Mimi. Your mother doesn't have much money."

"My mother got a huge settlement when my daddy died and again when the family sold the farm to Lord Farley."

"Unfortunately, your step-father went through it. Apparently he was a man with a gambling habit who always made the wrong bet. If he hadn't died when he did, your family would be destitute."

Hugh pulled his arm away from Mimi.

"She has the money you gave her," Mimi said.

"Do you really think she will spend any money on Hugh after the way he double-crossed her? I think not."

"My mother wouldn't shun me."

"Your mother asked me, as head of the family, to handle this situation as I saw fit, but there's a phone on the desk if you wish to call and verify."

Mimi stood, but hesitated going to the phone. "This is all your doing. You hate me because I'm younger and more beautiful."

"Shut up, Mimi, and sit down. Let me think," Hugh said, looking anxious.

"Don't you worry, Hugh. I have my own money," Mimi said.

"Sorry to burst your bubble, but as you are not of legal age, your mother signed a contract for you that contained a clause stipulating I could rescind payments into your account anytime. There will be no more money coming your way.

You will have to live on your earnings. In other words—work for your keep."

"You filthy swine. How can you do this to us after your own father was cast out because he loved someone the family disapproved of?"

"I thought about your situation being similar, but there are strong differences. My father was twenty-five years old and my mother twenty when they married. They had grown up together, so they knew each other's character, and could make their own way in the world, and as you said, my father gave up his fortune to marry my mother." Mona turned to Hugh. "You need to get a job. Perhaps a fresh start in Virginia where there are Thoroughbred farms needing a manager."

"Leave my family!" Mimi cried.

Hugh turned to Mimi. "Darling, let me handle this. Wait for me in the hallway. I want to speak to Mona alone. Please. Do it for me."

"If you think it best," Mimi replied, giving Hugh a curious look. "I'll be in the hallway if you need me."

"Thank you, my pet," Hugh said, making a kissing noise.

As soon as Mimi closed the library door, Hugh turned to Mona saying, "How much will you give me to go away?"

Ten minutes later, Hugh threw open the library door and walked out the house folding a check. One of the Pinkertons followed while the other restrained Mimi.

"Hugh? HUGH! HUGH!" Mimi cried. She pulled away from the Pinkerton man, and marched toward Mona who was standing in the library doorway holding her private checkbook.

Mimi pledged, "I'll never forgive you for this. I'll hate you until the day I die!"

"You will hate me for a long time, but maybe ten years from now when you are married to a man who really loves you, there might be forgiveness. Believe me, I take no pleasure in this."

"How much did you give him?"

"The amount Hugh asked for, and he readily agreed to my terms. There was no fight in him as with my father. He was not ready to sacrifice all for the woman he loved. Save yourself for someone worthy of you." Mona leaned against the doorjamb, feeling weak and sad. "This has been very trying. I need to rest. This gentleman will take you to your mother now. Melanie is waiting. Perhaps she can make you understand."

Mimi gave Mona one last loathsome look before leaving Moon Manor with the Pinkerton man.

Mimi's dark feelings gave Mona pause. Perhaps it would be best if Mimi was sent to a boarding school where she wouldn't be reminded of today's unpleasant events. Mona would discuss it later with Melanie. Right now, she was having trouble breathing and called for Jetta to phone Dr. Tuttle. She had barely uttered the words when everything went dark.

And stayed dark.

33

Mona awakened to Chloe licking her face. "What happened?"

"You fainted," Dr. Tuttle announced, putting his stethoscope into his bag. "One of the ribs you injured in the horse fall moved and was threatening your lungs. I think I prodded it back to where it belongs."

Mona groaned, "Gee, whatever you did hurts like the dickens."

"Each complaint about my work adds a dollar to your bill. Good day."

Violet opened the bedroom door to let the doctor out. "Miss Mona, Dr. Tuttle has left powder sedatives for you. Shall I fetch a glass of water?"

"Fill the water carafe by the bed, please. I'll

take one if I need to. Right now, I want to rest and possibly read the new mystery novel I purchased. It's by Erle Stanley Gardner and features his new hero, Perry Mason."

"You should not be straining your eyes."

"I'm going to relax today, but I shall be up and around tomorrow."

Violet looked as though she was going to ask something but decided against it.

"What is it, Violet?"

"It's my afternoon off, and I promised my mother I would help make cakes for her church's bazaar, but I don't want to leave you like this."

"I'll be fine. I am feeling much better."

"Really, Miss?"

"One should never renege on a promise to their mother."

"Oh, thank you, Miss." Violet beamed, giving Mona much encouragement in light of the horrid events of the morning.

"Get your hat. It looks like a storm is brewing."

"I'll be back before dark."

"Take your time. I can always ring for Mrs. Haggin."

"She's gone to visit her sister in Winchester."

"Hmm. Well, Samuel can see about me."

"He's at the picture show."

"Who is in the house?" Mona asked.

"Jed is cleaning the kitchen and Thomas is in his room, but Monsieur Bisaillon and Isaac have gone home."

"Obbie?"

"He went into town to get spices Monsieur Bisaillon needed, but he's going straight home afterwards, and Jed will be leaving shortly to join him."

"So it's just Thomas until Mrs. Haggin and Samuel return. Really, I'll be fine. The Doc has fixed me up. My breathing is much better. I have my mystery to read and Chloe is with me. I shall pass a quiet afternoon happily. If I need Thomas, I can ring the bell or holler into the heat registers," Mona teased.

"I don't know," Violet said, suddenly unsure about leaving Mona alone.

"Oh, Violet. Be off with you."

"If you say so. I'll only be three hours at the most. I'll check in on you when I get back." Violet hurried away leaving Mona in splendid quiet.

She puffed up her pillows and opened the comforter so Chloe could burrow under. A cheerful fire danced in the fireplace while the wind picked up outside. Mona took a deep breath, releasing tension due to the confrontation with Mimi and her Lothario. She hoped Mimi would understand the true nature of Hugh Beaumont one day and forgive her.

Feeling the bandages around her middle, Mona cursed her bad luck of being thrown from the mare. Her chest and sides were very tender, and the morning's relapse would further slow her inquiries. Mona shook her head as if to clear away the cobwebs. At the moment, she had a delicious afternoon all to herself, and she was going to enjoy it. Mona opened her book to read, and before long she drifted off to sleep without the aid of Dr. Tuttle's sedative.

34

Mona awoke to the sound of Chloe barking at the hallway door. "What's the matter, girl? Have to go potty?"

Chloe's barking intensified as she paced back and forth from the door to the bed.

Fully awake, Mona sniffed. "Oh, golly. Is that smoke I smell?" She jumped out of bed and was gripped by a stabbing pain in her side. Rushing to the door, she felt the wood. It was warm to the touch, and smoke was billowing from underneath the door into the room.

Grabbing the key, Mona ran into Violet's room in search of a safe exit. The hallway door was still cool to the touch. Mona hurriedly stuck the key in the lock, but it wouldn't turn. Something was jamming the lock!

Mona rushed back through the bathroom and turned on the tub. Throwing towels into the water, she took the wet towels and placed them under each door leading to the hallway. Picking Chloe up, she jumped into the shower and turned it on full blast getting them both drenched as much as possible in a few short seconds.

Dripping water on the floor, Mona returned to the master bedroom and pulled frantically on the servants' cord before going over to the heat register, screaming for help.

Not waiting to see if anyone would answer, Mona pulled the sheets off the bed and soaked them in the tub. As she was wrapping Chloe in a wet sheet, shouts and thudding sounded on the staircase. It was probably Thomas answering her ring only to discover the fire.

Mona cried, "Thomas, get a ladder. Meet me at the balcony. Not hearing a reply, Mona continued to tie sheets together. The room was filling with smoke regardless of the towels placed against the door, as the fire began to breach the inner wall.

Carrying Chloe onto the balcony, Mona peered over the rail. She was relieved to see no fire lashing out from the room beneath her.

Thomas and Jamison rushed around the corner of the house. In the distance, someone was ringing a great bell.

"Where's the ladder?" Mona yelled.

Thomas clapped his hand around his mouth and cried, "It will take a few minutes for the men to bring a tall ladder from the barns."

"I'm not waiting. Make ready for Chloe."

"Hold on a minute," Thomas hollered back. He ran into the house and came back out with a throw that had been on a couch in the library. He and Jamison spread out the throw tightly between them. "Ready."

Coughing, Mona's breathing became increasingly labored as smoke overtook the room. She hastily knotted wet sheets together into a makeshift rope and tied it around the trembling dog. "Trust me, Chloe. I'm going to get you out of this. Be calm, little girl. Be calm."

Fighting through the pain from her ribs, Mona heaved Chloe over the railing and lowered her to Thomas and Jamison.

"Drop her, Miss Mona. We've got her."

Seeing Chloe was safe, Mona looked around

in desperation. Where was the ladder?

Several farm hands gathered around conferring with Thomas and Jamison.

Thomas shouted, "The fire's on the second floor. Folks are throwing water on it, but it's pretty fierce."

"Get me out of here, Thomas!"

"Working on it. The tall ladders seem to be missing." He barked orders at some men who rushed off.

Gagging from the smoke, Mona grew desperate and decided her only hope was to climb over the railing and jump. She steadied herself on the narrow ledge outside the railing and was about to leap when a flatbed truck screeched under the balcony. Men jumped onto the truck bed and raised a ladder against the house. It didn't quite reach Mona, but if she hung over the railing, she might make contact with the first rung.

Big Sean, a burly Irishman from County Cork, climbed up the ladder while the other men held it. "Lass, come on. Just a wee bit more."

With her last bit of strength, Mona hung from the railing and struggled to find the ladder with her feet.

Reaching up, Big Sean grabbed Mona's legs. Thinking she was going to fall, Mona screamed, but Big Sean held fast and carried her down the ladder.

Jamison threw a blanket around Mona's shoulders and put her in the cab of the truck along with Chloe. Mona took off the poodle's wet sheet while Chloe licked Mona's face. "I know the feeling, Chloe." She turned to Jamison, "Thank you, Jamison."

"We've got to save Moon Manor. No time for thanks." He put the truck in gear and sped to the front driveway where farmhands had formed a line bringing out as much as they could. Mr. Gallo and his crew sprayed the house with water while others were on the staircase beating the fire out with burlap bags, rugs, anything they could find that might smother the flames. Others threw buckets of water.

But it was too little too late. The fire had spread to the entire west wing.

Mona grabbed hold of Jamison. "Is everyone out of the house? Miss Jetta? Mrs. Haggin?"

Jamison shook his head. "I don't know."

A car screeched to a halt in the driveway, and

Melanie jumped out dressed in an evening gown. Finding Mona, she clasped her in a tight embrace. "I was on my way to dinner at the Chestersons when I saw the fire over the treetops. Is everyone safe?"

"I don't know where Miss Jetta and Mrs. Haggin are, Melanie. I think Violet is at her mother's, but only Thomas of the house staff is accounted for."

"Miss Mona! Miss Melanie!"

Both women turned to see Violet climbing over a fence and rushing toward them.

"Violet, what a relief to know you're safe," Mona said.

"What happened?"

"I don't know, but it started on the second floor near the master suite."

Melanie and Violet exchanged concerned glances while Mona stared at the great house going up in flames.

Mona, Melanie, and Violet huddled together under a great pin oak tree, watching men trying to put out the fire. Finally, the fire trucks arrived and after an hour, the blaze was put out.

Dexter and Willie arrived with Dr. Tuttle.

Shock showed on their faces after seeing Moon Manor ruined. People were still bringing out anything they could and dumped items in the driveway while Thomas had the furniture loaded into trucks and taken to a nearby barn. Dirty, exhausted farm hands stood in clumps drinking water and smoking cigarettes. Women from the farm poured cups of hot coffee and distributed sandwiches or hoecakes slathered in jam, which the men gratefully accepted.

Several of the farmhands had been burned, and Violet's mother poured clean cool water on their wounds before binding them with strips of clean sheets until Dr. Tuttle could attend them. Violet left Mona and went to help her mother.

"Tarnation," Dr. Tuttle said, pointing a finger at Mona. "You sure are a lightning rod for trouble."

"It's not me causing the mischief, old man," Mona fired back. "Tend to your patients and keep a civil tongue in your head." She resented Tuttle's accusation.

Surprised at Mona's backtalk, Dr. Tuttle harrumphed and went off to treat the injured.

Willie held a weeping Melanie when Miles

wandered up behind them. "Oh, Mother, do quit making a fuss."

Melanie swirled around and slapped Miles' face. "Don't ever talk to me like that again. Don't you understand more than just a house has burned? My girlhood, my wedding to your father, memories of my mother and father have gone with it."

Rubbing his face, Miles uttered, "Gee, you are crackers."

Willie snapped, "Miles, go help instead of standing around. You're about as useless as a coal bucket without a handle."

"Mind your own business, Mrs. Deatherage."

"You're a worthless boy, that's for sure," Willie spat out.

When his mother didn't rise to his defense, Miles sulked away, looking for dropped trinkets in the driveway to stuff in his pocket.

"It's not his fault, Willie. I spoiled him and he's a pitiful boy because of it."

"If he doesn't shape up, Melanie, he'll come to no good."

"I know. I know." Melanie said, watching Mona walking over to them. Wiping away her tears, she put on a brave front.

Mona said, "Everything that can be done has been. Samuel is back now, and he and Thomas are staying at the house tonight. The downstairs wasn't touched, so they'll stay in their rooms. We are still trying to locate Mrs. Haggin and Jetta, but I'm sure they are safe. I remember something about Jetta having a hair appointment. Obadiah and Jedediah have been located at their family home. I don't think anyone was in the fire."

"It's a miracle you escaped," Willie said. "How did it start?"

"The fire chief is still investigating but he said it looked like an accelerant was used. Thomas said he smelled gasoline."

Thinking back to the morning's altercation, Melanie gasped, "Hugh Beaumont!"

"The police are looking for him. Look, I'm bushed. Violet and I are staying at the Phoenix Hotel until this is sorted out. Dexter has hired Pinkertons to guard the house and the horses. If it was arson, we don't want to take the chance it might happen again. I pray you both good night," Mona said.

Willie held out her hand. "Feel that?

Raindrops. Couldn't come at a better time."

Mona gave a tired, grimy smile. "Thank you, Wilhelmina, for looking on the bright side of this tragedy."

"What else can one do?" Willie replied.

Mona bid the ladies goodbye and called for Chloe. The poodle came bounding up, panting heavily from all the excitement. From the crumbs in her fur, Mona deduced Chloe had been begging food from the farm workers and firemen. It reminded Mona she hadn't eaten and was hungry. "Nothing like an emergency to get the old stomach juices flowing, eh, Chloe."

Jamison pulled the car up and jumped out. "Come on, Miss Mona. Let's get you settled in at the Phoenix. I need to get back and help. I'm staying in the house tonight with Thomas and Samuel. As soon as it's light, I'm checking every car and even the farm's vehicles. Gotta report back to Mr. Deatherage."

"The three of you need to rest. I insist upon it."

Jamison didn't have time to answer, as Violet emerged from the house with soot on her clothes and a rip in her stockings.

"Violet, what were you doing?"

"Trying to get some things together for us, but the firemen said the staircase wasn't safe and wouldn't let me pass."

"We can buy whatever we need in town. I hear the Phoenix has room service, so let's go before the kitchen shuts down. I'm starving."

Jamison opened the car door and Chloe jumped in followed by Violet. Lastly, Mona stepped in, still wearing wet clothes and swathed in a stinky horse blanket with no shoes.

She didn't care what people would think and was determined to walk with her head high through the main lobby to her suite. After all, she was Madeline Mona Moon, a cartographer by trade, explorer by nature, adventurer by heart—and someone had just tried to kill her—yet again.

35

Violet opened the door to the hotel suite. There stood Lord Farley with a bouquet of white roses.

"I'll see if Miss Mona is receiving."

"Don't bother. I'll announce myself," Farley said, pushing through and striding into an empty sitting room. "Where is she?"

"In the bedroom having breakfast, but don't go in," Violet said, but too late. Farley swung open the door and surprised Mona who was munching on a strip of bacon with Chloe inching her snout toward the breakfast tray.

"Don't you ever knock?" Mona complained.

"I got back into town last night and came here first thing this morning."

"Heard about the fire, I suppose?"

"My butler told me several days ago when I phoned home. Too bad. Can Moon Manor be restored?"

"Remains to be seen." Mona continued eating her breakfast, ignoring Farley.

He asked, "Are you going to offer me a chair?"

"No," Mona said, buttering her toast.

"Do you want to know where I've been? I've been gone for days."

"Not really," Mona said, taking a sip of coffee.

"Did you miss me?"

"Hardly," Mona said, feeding Chloe a morsel of bacon.

"This might change your cold, feckless heart," Farley said, tossing a piece of paper on the breakfast tray.

She picked it up, slowly reading. "Well, well. The last piece of the puzzle and you discovered it, Lord Farley. How good of you. Would you like a chair?"

"Don't mind if I do."

"Violet, get a vase for the roses. I expect they are for me."

Farley chuckled. "It's amazing how a woman

can turn on a dime when she gets what she wants."

"Not wants, Farley. Needs. With this I'm going to throw some mud on the wall and see what sticks."

"May I be present?"

"Assuredly."

"Oh, goody."

"What made you think of it?"

"Elimination, my fair maiden. Had to be someone with authority, access, and will."

"Here's to your good health, Lord Farley. May you always be my friend, and never my enemy. Would you like a piece of toast?"

"You're too kind."

"Aren't I though," Mona replied, beaming and feeling quite smug and victorious.

Farley had just handed Mona the final piece of the puzzle, and she was going to use it as a cudgel and hit someone over the head with it.

36

Mona called a meeting in her suite at the Phoenix Hotel a month after the fire. Her ribs had healed, and all bruising had disappeared. She looked smart in a silver-gray suit and white blouse, the colors highlighting her platinum hair. She wore a simple strand of pearls and no earrings. Only a Tiffany tank watch graced one wrist.

Melanie came with the Deatherages since she and Willie had kissed and made-up at the fire. Miles showed up with Archer in tow.

Mrs. Haggin and Miss Jetta arrived with Jamison, Thomas, and Samuel bringing up the rear.

The doorbell rang again. Violet answered the door, letting in Lord Farley who handed over his coat, hat, and walking stick before greeting everyone with a big hello.

Thomas helped Violet serve tea until Mona asked for quiet.

"I have some important news to impart, and thought it best to have everyone together when I announced it, so I don't have to repeat myself and answer any questions you might have," Mona declared, standing before her seated guests. "Mr. Deatherage has worked with the insurance company, and they will reimburse us for the rewiring and plumbing plus paint, flooring, and such. The insurance company also gave us an allowance for replacing the furniture, but they will not pay for what they consider cosmetic embellishments. That is on us. Since the house was built in 1892 and has only minor renovations to accommodate electricity and modern plumbing, I am ordering a complete overhaul of Moon Manor. I hope to have a brighter and more modern ancestral home, bringing the mansion out of the Victorian age and up to current building codes."

Most of the staff clapped.

"Workmen have already cleared the debris

and will start work shortly. Most of the damage was near the master suite on the second floor. After working on a budget with Mr. Deatherage, it has been decided a servants' elevator will be installed on the end of the west wing and an additional bathroom with a shower will be built in the downstairs near the kitchen. The men will have their own bathroom, and the female staff will have a private space to tidy up and put on their lipstick."

Miss Jetta and Violet chuckled.

"As below, so above. I'm paraphrasing that a little bit. The third floor bathroom will be modernized. Since the bedrooms on the third floor are small and Moon Manor doesn't employ the number of staff it used to, all the bedrooms will be enlarged with a common sitting room for all the female staff to enjoy." Mona looked around, noticing Violet and Miss Jetta beaming.

Only Mrs. Haggin looked sour and spoke up. "Will the current staff retain their positions?"

"There's going to be a change in staffing, I must admit."

"May I be informed of the changes?" Mrs. Haggin asked.

"Assuredly, Mrs. Haggin, but let me speak of the investigation into the fire. I know you have heard rumors concerning the origin of the fire. Thomas, did you speak with the fire chief?"

"Yes'am. I told him I smelled gasoline when I ran up the stairs. The carpets and the wallpaper were on fire near the top of the steps. That's why I couldn't get to you, Miss Mona."

"Your observations proved to be correct. The fire was deliberately set with gasoline poured on the second floor hallway carpet and walls. It is believed the culprit set the fire and then made his way down the stairs and out the front door."

"Who would do such a thing?" Melanie asked.

"Someone who wanted me out of the way. Someone who wanted the Moon fortune for himself. Miles, what do you have to say about this?"

Miles jumped up. "Are you accusing me? I never set that fire."

"Sit down, dear. You're making a scene," Melanie cautioned with glee.

Mona said, "You've never masked your bitterness that your mother was not the principal heir."

"Who wouldn't be? No one knew of your existence before you arrived. You are not part of this family. The money should have gone through Mother and then to me."

"I was known. Your mother knew of me, and Uncle Manfred kept in contact with my mother."

Miles scoffed, "Your mother! A gardener's daughter."

"The wife of the intended heir of Moon Manor—Mathias Milton Moon, my father. The line of inheritance has been corrected with his daughter being restored to the family bosom."

"There has been nothing but disaster since you came," Miles said.

"Did you have anything to do with Manfred Moon's fall down the staircase?"

"It's no secret I wanted our uncle to die. I was in need of money, and he was in the way, but I didn't cause him to croak."

"How charmingly put," Willie muttered.

Mona said, "I think Uncle Manfred's fall and the brake failures on his cars were premeditated."

"I had nothing to do with that. It's not my fault if an old man stumbles down some stairs, or Jamison is negligent."

Jamison angrily rose from his chair and said, "Somebody tampered with those cars. They were in good working order. I'll swear on the Bible."

Mona held up her hand. "I think the fall was caused by fishing line strung across the stairwell, and in the dark, Manfred didn't see it. That's why the lights were turned off."

Thomas spoke up, "There was no such wire when Samuel and I got there."

"I believe that the same person who left the wire across the stairs and tampered with the cars, also put the burr under my horse blanket and set the fire to Moon Manor."

"You aren't going to pin this on me!" Miles shouted. "Yes, I wanted Uncle Manfred dead, but I've never hurt anyone in my life."

"Mona, you can't really believe Miles killed Uncle Manfred," Melanie said.

Mona said, "No, I don't."

"That's a relief," Melanie said.

"But I think he was involved whether he knew it or not."

Miles sputtered, "I wish you'd go away and leave us in peace."

"Very well then. Since you feel so adamant, I'll

give you and your mother a choice. Melanie, I will be happy to hand over the reins of Moon Manor and all that goes with it. Mr. Deatherage will work out the minor details such as my annual remittance, but you will have the bulk of the estate. What say you?"

"Mother, take it. Take it. Now is our chance," Miles begged.

Melanie hesitated.

"MOTHER! Do as I say!"

A look of irritation showed on Melanie's face. "Miles, I'm sick of being hounded by men, and I will not tolerate it from my son. First it was my bully of a father. Then both my husbands and every man I've met in between. Melanie, do this. Melanie, I need money. Melanie. Melanie. Melanie. Blah, blah, blah. Even the lawsuit was your idea. I never wanted to sue."

"It got us some money, didn't it? Now I can go out with the fellows and hold my head up high."

"You mean pay for your friends' tab at speak-easies and bet on the ponies."

"That's part of college life."

"It's part of being played for a fool by your friends."

244

"Mother, please. We're nobodies without the money."

Willie declared, "That's a very sad thing to say about oneself."

Melanie said, "Mona, you stay as head of the Moon family. I would only lose the fortune to some flimflam man or Miles would spend it at the track." She turned to Miles. "It may be too late for you, son, but it's not for Mimi. I'm going to send her away from all this temptation, and if God is merciful, he'll show her to the other side of her broken heart."

Miles sank in his seat.

Mona spoke up. "This doesn't settle the matter of whether Miles set the fire or not."

"Why would I set fire to a house I wanted to inherit? Makes no sense," Miles said.

"Exactly, which is why I struck you off the list. Let's start at the beginning of this tawdry tale. The Moon family has faced several tragedies over the past thirteen months."

"It began with Mr. Moon's discovery of the embezzling," Miss Jetta said.

Mona corrected her. "It started months before that, and it has to do with you, Archer."

Archer looked surprised. "Me? I'm a valet and nothing more. I could never inherit the Moon money."

"But you could steal from it."

"I never stole anything."

"Your wife did."

"You're off your head. I have no wife."

"But you do, Archer. I have a marriage certificate via Lord Farley, documenting that you were married two years ago in Clark County to a Helen Martha Jackson."

Archer remained silent with his head bowed.

"Archer?"

"I have nothing to say."

"Would you, Mrs. Haggin?"

Indignant, Mrs. Haggin said, "Are you implying I am married to Archer?"

"I'm not implying anything. I am stating as fact that you are the wife of Archer and a thief who has been lining her pockets for years with Moon money until you got too greedy and Manfred Moon discovered your treachery."

"You claim this marriage certificate says he married a Helen Martha Jackson. My name is Mrs. Haggin."

"Housekeepers are commonly referred to as a 'missus' regardless of marital status, and Mrs. Haggin is a pseudonym because you didn't want people to know Helen Jackson had been picked up for shoplifting in Winchester as a young woman. Helen Jackson would never had gotten employment in any respectable house with a police record, so Mrs. Haggin was born. Knowing you had family in Winchester and based on a hunch, Lord Farley researched the marriage licenses at the courthouse until he found Archer's name. Believing you to be Archer's bride, he interviewed your relatives who testified to the existence of your marriage and signed statements stating thus. I have their sworn affidavits here."

"So what. I married and kept it a secret. It's not a crime to keep one's personal life private."

"But theft is."

Mrs. Haggin protested, "I have no idea what you are talking about. It's rubbish, pure and simple."

"One of the tasks I assigned Mr. Deatherage was a complete audit of all the household accounts going back five years. We found all the food accounts were excessively padded with you and the vendors taking a cut off the top."

"Mr. Bisaillon handles the kitchen. You should take your accusations to him."

"We did. We also got records of his bank account. Normal deposits. We monitored how he lived. No purchases out of the ordinary. He said you handled the food accounts."

"He lies."

"Would Obadiah and Jedediah, good Christian boys, lie as well? I think not. All three men said the same thing. Mr. Bisaillon always turned the receipts over to you."

"Mr. Moon paid the household accounts. Not me."

"Yes, but he was not aware the food bills had a twenty percent markup. The grocer, the butcher, the milkman would get paid and give you a kickback of ten percent while they put the other ten percent directly in their pockets."

Mrs. Haggin tried to defend her actions. "Mr. Moon never gave me a raise in my years of service. Anytime I asked for more money, he would dismiss the idea out of hand, but he'd spend a fortune on those stupid horses, while I had to beg for a new apron. It's an open secret housekeepers do this type of thing all the time. We're forced to do so. Our employers certainly don't look after us."

"Did that include selling wine and bourbon from the Moon cellars? Mr. Deatherage had the original inventory for the liquor when Uncle Manfred went on a spending spree before Prohibition. Even with daily use of wine and entertaining from time to time, bottles of rare wine are missing as well as entire cases of bourbon and gin."

"You can't prove I stole any spirits. Perhaps Monsieur Bisaillon takes a nip. After all, he has a key to the cellar as well."

"I can prove you progressed from petty thief to major embezzler."

"I'm not going to sit here and be insulted like this. I've given twenty years to the Moon family, and this is the thanks I get." She jumped up and rushed the door, but Lord Farley blocked her way.

"Better sit down, Mrs. Haggin. Miss Mona is not finished yet," he suggested.

Mrs. Haggin, seeing the way to freedom futile, groaned and sat beside Archer.

Willie slid a flask from her purse, took a healthy swig, and croaked, "This is better than any mystery playing on the radio. Who knew our Mona was so clever?"

"Where was I?" Mona said. "Oh yes, I am trying to construct a timeline of the events. The deadly sin of greed took over more and more until you began writing checks as well, forging my uncle's signature. It was a couple dollars at first until the amounts were staggering, and Uncle Manfred finally caught on in December 1931. You were very clever to make your handwriting look like Melanie's in case there was a discovery."

"It was you! You got me thrown out of my home because of your duplicity," Melanie sputtered at Mrs. Haggin.

Mona added, "After December, 1931 there were no more checks written by you."

Mrs. Haggin insisted, "Because Miss Melanie was thrown out on her ear. No more access to her brother's checkbook."

"It was because the jig was up, and you didn't dare forge another check. Besides, Uncle Manfred entrusted the checkbook to Mr. Deatherage."

"I never cashed any of those checks. They went to legitimate out-of-town firms."

"It would be interesting to learn how you know that, but the same deal was made with them as with local vendors. They received checks for phony invoices and once cashed, would wire your cut back to your private account."

Mrs. Haggin sat defiantly with her arms crossed. "You can't prove a thing. All conjecture. It was Melanie who was accused by Manfred Moon, and she who was thrown out of the house. All you have is a marriage license."

Mona ignored Mrs. Haggin's outburst. "Then you found out Uncle Manfred had left you and Archer a small bequest in his will, amounting to only a few thousand, but a king's ransom these days. So how to get your hands on it? Manfred was in good health and only in his fifties, so you began planting insidious thoughts in people's minds, declaring he was acting feeble both mentally and physically."

"I deny it."

"Of course you do, but I'll continue. Now you bring Archer into your web. You had Archer tamper with the brakes on the two cars Uncle

Manfred used. If your treachery was discovered, Jamison would be blamed for incompetence since he serviced both cars. It would be easy to accuse Jamison of forgetting to check the brake lines. Well, that didn't work, but fortunately for you, Uncle Manfred caught the dreaded flu, but he still didn't die. Then he got pneumonia, and again, he wouldn't die, so you decided to have him fall down the stairs by tripping him with fishing line. You drugged the night nurse, dismantled the servants' bell, and sabotaged the hall lights. The coup de grace was when Manfred woke up with heartburn from the spicy dinner, which you served him. He wanted some bicarbonate. The nurse was asleep and no one responded to his ring, so Uncle Manfred decided to go to the kitchen where the bicarbonate was kept. Only he didn't see the fishing line because the lights weren't working and tumbled down the staircase. Archer conveniently was the first person on the scene to remove the line and make sure Manfred was dead. I guess the plan was for Archer to break my uncle's neck if still alive, but Thomas and Samuel arrived at the scene, making it impossible."

Mona retrieved a stack of photographs from an end table and threw them at Mrs. Haggin and Archer. "Here are photos of the holes in the stairwell and banister where the line was attached."

"I know nothing about this," Mrs. Haggin complained. "If Archer did this, he did it of his own accord. I was upstairs in my room asleep."

"Helen," Archer croaked, sounding wounded.

"I came along and started shaking things up. I wasn't compliant like Melanie. You saw with the argument over the master suite that I was not going to be easy to handle and might discover your thieving, so I had to go as well. Was it your plan, Archer, to sneak into my room and smother me with a pillow on the night of my arrival? When you weren't able to pull it off, the next was to have my head bashed in by a crazed horse. It would be easy to direct attention to either Miles or Hugh Beaumont as the culprit. Finally, the fire at Moon Manor. Was the plan to burn me out or just burn me? It was easy to gather information from either Miles or the servants who knew everything I was doing. It was so easy. You knew where I was at all times."

"I was with Mr. Miles, and he can account for my whereabouts," Archer said.

"And I was with my sister, so I couldn't have set the fire," Mrs. Haggin insisted.

"You said you were going to Winchester, but hid in the back garden shed, Mrs. Haggin. It was perfect timing for most of the servants were gone for the day. You crept back into the house and gummed up my bedroom locks with glue, then scattered gasoline in the hallway, lit it, and made your way to the back of the farm where your sister picked you up with her car. Burl will testify that you never left by the main gate."

"There are many ways to leave Mooncrest Farm. One doesn't have to go by the main gate, besides this is all circumstantial. No evidence whatsoever. You've got nothing on us."

"What you say is true, but the police have been notified and are currently investigating. I'm sure they'll get someone to talk. As for the two of you, you both are fired with no references. Thomas has already packed your things, and your luggage is waiting for you downstairs behind the front desk. If I see either one of you near my family or property again, or even if I just see you,

I'll sic the dogs on you. Now get out."

Thomas went to open the door and slammed it shut after Mrs. Haggin and Archer hurried out. "Good riddance to trash."

"I couldn't agree with you more," Willie concurred.

Farley sidled up to Mona. "Well done, old girl. Well done."

Violet asked, "Shall I open the champagne now?"

"Yes, and everyone listen. Let's drink to 1933 and to Mr. Roosevelt. May he guide us out of the darkness and into peace and prosperity."

"Hear. Hear," everyone chimed in, grabbing flutes of cold bubbly.

"To a chicken in every pot," Violet toasted.

Mona laughed. "Wrong administration, my dear, but I agree with the sentiment."

Violet grinned and took a big swig of the champagne. Working with Miss Mona was going to change her life.

She just knew it.

37

Mona strolled beside Mr. Gallo in quiet reflection, listening to him reminisce about her maternal grandfather and mother.

"Mrs. Moon wanted a whimsical garden for her children. Very popular gardens during the Edwardian period, so your grandfather designed these topiaries of bunnies, curious foxes, and galloping ponies. It was great fun to have picnics here. The staff's children were often included in these outings."

"It's nice to think my mother enjoyed Moon Manor."

"She did and was a favorite with Mrs. Moon."

"Did she oppose my parents' marriage, Mr. Gallo?"

"It was Mr. Moon senior. He believed a marriage between his oldest son and a gardener's daughter would stain the family's prestige. I think he bitterly regretted his decision after Mr. Mathias left, but was too proud to do anything about it. He died a broken man."

Knowing her grandfather regretted his decision about her parents made Mona feel better. "Mr. Gallo, can you make the grounds look as they did when my mother lived here? She loved flowers and fountains. I want to hear the sound of flowing water. Would you like to try?"

"I can make Mooncrest Farm the showpiece of the South."

"Then do it, Mr. Gallo. I would like to imagine Mother and Father walking hand-in-hand through the garden, young and untroubled."

"You can't undo the past, Miss Mona, but maybe your mother might want you to walk with a young man, untroubled in the garden."

"You don't have any prospects in mind for me, do you?"

"Lord Farley looks mighty keen."

"So he tells me, but I don't know. He's not my cup of tea."

"He might grow on you yet."

Mona laughed. "Like a fungus?"

"Even the tiniest seed can grow into a mighty tree. Give it time."

Mona heeded Mr. Gallo's words, but there was no rush. It was the gloaming of the evening and a soft yellow light filtered beyond the trees. Chloe trotted beside Mona as they made their way back to the house. She could hear Obbie fussing with Monsieur Bisaillon in the kitchen, Violet humming on the balcony while sewing a loose button, and horses neighing from nearby fields. The tranquility of Moon Manor was enough for now.

Madeline Mona Moon was happy at last.

Author's Notes

The history is true as are the politicians,
horsemen, and jockeys.

WWI was referred to as the Great War as WWII
hadn't occurred yet.

The 1933 Kentucky Derby Race is one of the
most famous horse races of all time. The true
winner is still being debated. You can see the race
on YouTube. You decide who the true
winner was.

Union Terminal in Cincinnati opened in 1933 and
is now a museum. Much of the original art work
remains, but many of the fabulous murals have
been relocated to the Cincinnati Airport.

The Moon family and Moon Manor are
fabrications of my imagination. So is Lord
Farley—'tis a shame though.

The wingding throughout the story is an ancient
alchemy symbol for copper—kind of goes with
the copper mines, the source of the Moon wealth.

You're not done yet.
Read on for a bonus chapter
from Mona's new adventure!
UNDER A BLOOD MOON

Mona has a new adventure.
This time she's going to Merry Old England!
An exciting new mystery by Abigail Keam.

Peek at the bonus chapter on the next page!

1

Madeline Mona Moon sat on the verandah overlooking her four thousand acre horse farm in Lexington, Kentucky, eating buttermilk biscuits slathered in gravy and eggs sunny side up with bacon on the side. It was going to be a busy day. She had an appointment with her lawyer, Dexter Deatherage, to sign legal papers regarding the Moon Enterprises copper mines. Then she was going to tour the farm with her new estate manager. Some of the white plank fences had grown a tad shabby, but Mona wasn't looking forward to the inspection. Repairing and repainting the fences would be time consuming and expensive, but it had to be done.

Her social secretary, Jetta Dressler, poured coffee for them both before going through the morning mail.

"Anything interesting?" Mona asked, reaching under the table to pet Chloe, her standard poodle.

Chloe smelled the bacon and nudged Mona with her wet nose.

Mona broke a crisp piece in two and fed Chloe half. "That's all you get, little missy. Samuel has already fed you your morning breakfast." Mona looked up to find Jetta giving her an impatient stare. "Sorry. You were saying."

Jetta handed over the morning mail. "Just some social invitations and a request to speak at the Lexington Women's Club in July."

"On what subject?"

"They want to hear about your adventures in Mesopotamia."

"I can't think of anything more boring."

Jetta smiled. "Surely, you can think of something to say—a single woman, carrying a handgun for protection, working in a foreign country surrounded by dangerous, exotic men. That in itself would be interesting to most women weighed down by the drudgery of their everyday routine. They're dying to hear from a woman who has actually experienced life."

"They want to know if I was swept up by a dashing sheik on a white charger and spirited into the desert for a romantic interlude like in some picture they saw with Rudolf Valentino."

"Well?"

"And if I rode a camel."

"Let's get back to the handsome sheik."

"I rode a donkey."

"Let's get back to the handsome sheik."

"All I saw were poor, desperate people oppressed by the Ottomans and then the British. They had nothing on their minds but survival."

"Why do you always have to be so practical, so blunt? I wish I could be swept away by some sheik to his private tent for a little canoodling."

"You'd have to share him with his other three wives."

"What?"

"Muslim men are allowed four wives."

"I don't think I'd like that."

Mona grinned. "Be careful what you wish for, Jetta, if it concerns handsome dark-haired men with lascivious designs."

"Like the attractive Lord Farley?"

"What brought his name up?"

"Lord Farley is always bringing you flowers and candy. Those are pretty strong indications he wants to formally court you."

"Phsaw. You make it sound like Farley wants to go steady and pin my sweater. He just wants a new notch on his belt. Well, I'll not give him the satisfaction. He'll tire of chasing me sooner or later and try his luck with some other filly."

"If you say so, but he looks mighty determined."

"Let's talk about something else, shall we? How are the repairs to Moon Manor coming along?" asked Mona, referring to the remodeling of her ancestral home after a fire devastated the west wing of the mansion. The cause of the fire had been declared arson by the police, and Mona's previous housekeeper, Mrs. Haggin, had been arrested for the fire. She had also been indicted as a conspirator in the murder of Manfred Michael Moon, Mona's uncle. Mrs. Haggin's husband, Archer, fled before he could be arrested. Mona hoped she had seen the last of his backside forever.

Jetta looked at her notes. "The servants' elevator for the west wing is going to be installed this week. Once installed, they will build the encasement around it."

"Do they have the correct stone?"

"The material will arrive tomorrow, and it is a match for Moon Manor's existing masonry. In fact, it came from the same quarry in Indiana."

"Same color?"

"Exactly the same," Jetta repeated. She was well aware that Mona worried about making a mistake restoring Moon Manor. Jetta thought she was right to be concerned. Many of the locals considered Mona an outsider, and worse, a Yankee. Some Bluegrass stalwarts would be happy for Mona to fall on her face. The sight of a rich and powerful newcomer making a fool of herself would reinforce their dislike of outsiders. It didn't matter that Mona employed over a hundred people and kept them from poverty's door during the Depression, or she began a health program to rid her workers' children of lice, rickets, and worms—common childhood ailments during the 1930s. All they saw was that Mona was chauffeured about in a red and black Daimler during the week, but didn't go to church on Sunday, even with a driver to take her. Shame. Shame.

While tongues wagged behind Mona's back, everyone was polite after hearing the rumor she kept a gun in her purse and would shoot anyone who looked at her cross-eyed. How folks knew Mona kept a pistol on her person, Jetta didn't know, but she suspected Mona's Aunt Melanie might have played a part in spreading the gossip.

Jetta eyed Mona eating her breakfast. The sun filtered through the trees highlighting Mona's platinum hair and fair skin, giving her an ethereal quality. Even Mona's golden eyes lent her otherworldliness hard to describe unless one saw it for herself. She knew Mona must realize what people were whispering, but she didn't seem to care, as Mona's facial expression was always one of composure and confidence.

For a moment, Jetta wished she could be more like Mona, but she let her behavior be dictated by others' opinions too often. She was determined to emulate Mona and steer her own future, but Jetta's thoughts were disturbed by Violet, Mona's personal maid, carrying a small silver tray, hurrying out on the verandah.

"Miss Mona, a telegram has come for you," Violet said, breathlessly and obviously dying of curiosity to know what the telegram contained.

Mona picked up the telegram and noticed Violet had stationed herself where she could read it when opened. "Thank you, Violet. That will be all."

"You might need to answer it, Miss Mona. The messenger boy is waitin'."

Mona grinned. "All right, Violet. Can I read it by myself first, though?"

Violet stepped back, waiting impatiently. Telegrams were exciting, and Violet wished she would get one someday. She had only received two letters in her entire life and secretly wished for a pen pal from the other side of the world.

"Oh, no!"

"What is it, Miss Mona?" Jetta said, alarmed at Mona's distraught expression. She had never seen Mona so upset.

Mona handed her the telegram. "It's from my friend, Lady Alice Morrell. She says her life is in danger and I should come at once."

"Does she say why?" Jetta asked, picking up the telegram and reading it.

"I must go to her. She would never send such a message if she wasn't in real need." Mona turned to Violet, who quivered with anticipation. "Violet, have Thomas bring up my steamer trunks. Pack them quickly. I'll keep my appointment with Mr. Deatherage, but when I get back, we'll have Jamison drive us immediately to Cincinnati to catch the express train to New York."

"Us, Miss?"

"I certainly can't go to England without my maid. Whatever you don't have, we'll either purchase on the ship or in London."

"I'm going across the ocean . . . with you?"

Mona turned to Jetta. "I'll need you to make travel arrangements."

"It's very short notice, but I'll do what I can," Jetta replied, a little flustered. She had never made transcontinental preparations before.

"You must do more than that. You must take over the mansion repairs and the running of the farm. Do you think you're up for it?"

"I can try."

"You must do more than try. You must succeed. Of course, you may wire me if you need assistance. Mr. Deatherage will handle all my routine business concerns, but he will help you carry through."

"If you insist."

"I must. There's much to do before I travel this afternoon, so I'll leave you now." Mona stood and gathered the telegram from Jetta. "Violet, close your mouth and move."

"Yes, Miss. Right away, Miss." Violet scampered off to find Thomas, the butler.

Jetta said, "Miss Mona, the Western Union boy is waiting for an answer."

Mona's cheeks grew a healthy pink color. "I must respond to Lady Alice. Thank you for reminding me." She hurried to the front hall and found the messenger waiting patiently.

"Any message, Miss?" he asked, doffing his hat.

"Just say this. 'Amiens.'"

"Amen, Miss?"

"No. A M I E N S."

"Is it a who or a what, if you don't mind my asking?"

"Amiens is where the Allied forces launched a counterattack against the Germans in 1918. It was the beginning of the end for the Great War."

"The telegram boy stood dumbfounded. He

had written many an odd message in his time, but this was very peculiar. "Yes, but what does it mean?"

"I'm coming!"

You can check out all the fabulous people and locations mentioned in the Mona Moon Mysteries on my Pinterest board for **The Mona Moon Mysteries**

The Josiah Reynolds Mysteries

Josiah Reynolds is a beekeeper who loves her bees, her art collection, and a one-eyed Mastiff named Baby. She lives at the edge of a cliff on the Kentucky Palisades in a mid-century marvel called the Butterfly. She has everything–money, a great husband, lots of friends–until one day she loses it all. Now Josiah's broke, divorced, and discovers she has a knack for finding dead bodies in the land of Thoroughbreds, bourbon, and antebellum mansions where secrets die hard and the past is never past.

The Last Chance For Love Series

After her divorce, Eva Hanover leaves New York City and heads for the Florida Keys. She buys a rundown motel in the seediest part of Key Largo, intending to restore it to its mid-century glory. As Eva refurbishes the motel, the magic of love returns and guests find a second chance at life.

The Princess Maura Tales

Princess Maura must fight and destroy Dorak, the Aga of Bhuttania, in order to free her people from tyranny. She must put aside her own feelings to win a war and restore order, even if it means killing the great love of her life. Danger, romance, and adventure follow Maura as she navigates the treacherous world of Kaseri where evil wizards morph into dragons, a mysterious race of bird-people train her to be a warrior, and an ancient plant gives her magical powers to overcome her enemies.

About The Author

Please don't forget to leave a review at place of purchase and tell your friends about Mona.

Join my mailing list at: www.abigailkeam.com

Join my VIP FB – Abigail's Queen Bees

You can also reach me at Instagram, Twitter, Goodreads, YouTube, and Pinterest.

Thank you again, gentle reader, for your review, which is so important for any book. I hope to meet you again between the pages.

CPSIA information can be obtained
at www.ICGtesting.com
Printed in the USA
LVHW030301261119
638451LV00011B/936/P